Alan Fraser is an international development consultant, at present, working in Kenya. He was with the UN in New York for eight years and maintains a home in Westchester County for his estranged family. He is domiciled in Scotland.

Born in the British military sector of Berlin, he spent his formative years in West Germany. After his German mother left him, he grew up in Edinburgh. He ran away from his domineering father, joining the army as a private (back to his childhood environment!). He fought his way to university, married and had four children.

Exploration

ALAN FRASER

Exploration

Chimera

CHIMERA PAPERBACK

© Copyright 2016
Alan Fraser

A CIP catalogue record for this title is
available from the British Library.

ISBN 978 190 313 657 7

Chimera is an imprint of
Pegasus Elliot MacKenzie Publishers Ltd.
www.pegasuspublishers.com

First Published in 2016

Chimera
Sheraton House Castle Park
Cambridge England

Printed & Bound in Great Britain

To those who seek to live a genuine life,
no matter how hard that sometimes proves to be.

1.

February 1, 1999.

Simone,

Let me tell you about my children, as I feel myself sinking into the mire of concern about things fundamental to survival. As you know, the very thought of such little ones was alien to my very being. The thought sent shudders through me and when it appeared on a woman's agenda, intentionally or not, openly or not, that was it. The shutters came down, emotionally and even visually, no matter how delicious the particular person was. I was not able to countenance such things. I was simply not willing to make a mess of others as others had made such a mess of me (from which the reverberations still strike deep, deep down into my subconscious).

Graham is now ten. He is handsome, lithe, precocious, and argumentative – with a great sense of humour. He will be a very good lawyer or journalist or broadcaster. Just now, he wants to be a movie director. I try and teach him the beauty of black and white movies! We have good fun. He came without trying! Moira after five years. Why? We were trying! Fun while we tried but increasingly frightening. She is now five and both demonstrative and athletic.

Andrew appeared without trying. When the pregnancy was announced, I was scared at the impact of such a thing. The dreadful thought occurred to us for a second. It was unthinkable. If we believed in some Almighty or other, surely he would never forgive us or me. The thought was banished and he was born, beautifully and naturally. His own challenges (severe Down's syndrome) have weighed most heavily on us since we realised something was amiss but we forge on, knowing that at times he has been the straw that has almost broken us, as human beings, let alone as parents or a married couple.

The times to be treasured now are from dinner time onwards – dominated by the children. We sit at the table (still trying to impart notions of decency and good manners). The meal finishes and things are cleared up (the children help sometimes). More general fun and games follow. As the first two play in some room or other, I take little Andrew, now two, up for a bath, around seven p.m. I kneel on the floor by the bath as he splashes and mumbles to himself and me – looking, playing and splashing. Eye contact has increased significantly since the turn of this year. Fifteen to twenty minutes later, he stands for me and I wrap a towel around him. I hold him close and squeeze him gently. I kiss him on his ear and he smiles. I dress him and take him downstairs, handing him to Heather. I also help Moira get her pyjamas on. She is good at getting ready for bed.

I take her because it is a time to treasure forever. I tuck

her into bed. She puts her arms out lovingly and tells me she loves me and sometimes pleads with me to sleep next to her. I tell her that I must help with Graham and Andrew. She takes the full length of my arm and hugs it (I think) pretending it is my body. I kiss and cuddle her until she is settled. What a treasured soul she is. How I must care for her and prepare her for the bruises of life yet to come, hoping that I form her into an emotionally resilient young person. She falls asleep soon after the hug.

Graham comes next. Getting him to change and wash is something of an ordeal, but ultimately, he never refuses. He just wants to have some time alone with his mum and dad. He had us to himself for five years and, we think, has never really adjusted to these others appearing and claiming attention. But he is a well-balanced soul. After supper he insists that one of us accompany him to the bathroom. I try and do it. We go up and he starts joking and laughing and describing ridiculous situations to me. I tell him to be quiet because the others are trying to sleep. He laughs quietly then settles down. I take him to bed, tuck him in, and kiss him (but for how much longer I wonder).

"I love you, Dad!"

"I love you, Graham. Sleep well!" He settles to slumber very quickly.

John and Heather then settle, usually watching TV, before she announces that she is tired and will go to bed. John makes his usual excuses about wanting to stay up, to watch some movie or other, or just to contemplate life. He will say anything or do anything to avoid going to bed at the same time. In fact, he hopes, each night, that she is asleep before he climbs into bed, clinging as close to his side as he can.

This sample of family life, in truth, the reality, was about six months into his *Exploration*. What on earth motivated him down this path?

2.

John's mind was not of this place. He was now out of work, having returned home from three years in East Africa. He had his young family with him. His wife, Heather, was struggling to cope with life in these circumstances – three young children, one of whom was disabled. She was silent in an effort to get through each day. He needed to talk. He needed an external source for such conversations.

By chance, he discovered Yahoo Personals. To him, the common thread of its advertisements was a cry for help. He entered his 'cry', ensuring that his potential market would be on a different continent; he in Europe, her in the USA. 'Yes', it had to be a woman.

His advertisement referred to his own autobiographical writing; would anyone be interested in reading such material? Replies came and he whittled them down to one.

February 2.

John,

Thank you for your e-mail. Well, I am surprised that your friends refused the idea of sharing thoughts via cyberspace. I find the premise of male/female friendship very complex.

I think it would be better if I got to know you before I read your material. I have been looking for pen pals with which to discuss books, so your ad caught my interest.

Let us start with you telling me a bit about who you are. Tell me about your education and whatever else you would like to share with me. I am a thirty-two-year-old mother of two. I have been very well educated in computer programming. I am picking up from where I left off ten years ago as far as reading material, other than technical manuals.

Thank you.
Simone.

February 2.
Simone,

I selected two possible friends from my past. One was American (my first choice). The other was British but with an international flavour – The Netherlands and South Africa, with encounters in both. I was disheartened to get conventional retorts. Then I discovered Yahoo Personals and its host of advertisements. Many seemed to yearn for the unreachable. Others were a little tawdry. Some simmered with potential. I couldn't believe I found such a variety in the human condition in such short amount of time.

Also, the absence of a physical reality; the notion of dealing in the purity of ideas has great attraction, intellectually and even, possibly, emotionally. It seems to be a sort of therapeutic experience but without the nuisance of a therapist.

I am, therefore, approaching this entire exploration from from the standpoint that neither of us inhabits this world, that we are not caught in the trappings of a physical reality. My original approach to my two former female friends – separately and sequentially – was founded on that premise. I suppose for me, now, this is the growing realization that my mother, who I never really knew, had a profound and perhaps disturbing influence on me through her absence. She left me when I was five, just before I started school. The memory is vivid. It remains so because, over the past two years, I have been writing autobiographically (but in the third person) in every spare moment available. It is a thing I have wanted to do for many years but only felt capable of doing so recently. There are thirty-five chapters in three volumes.

Thanks,

John.

February 4.

John,

I took half a day off. Yes, it is such a blessing to not be caught in the trappings of physical reality. I found this idea of yours very deep and true. Did I always think that way, or did I grow to think that way? I have actually just come to think that way. The past ten years of my life have been really strange. I stand today at a crossroads where I am examining the meaning of it all. I was struck by your comment about your mother and the age of separation. The reason is that I am about to be separated from my son, who is four years old, and it is so hard. I look at him every day and wonder if he will hate me for giving him up. I tell myself that I am not giving him up forever and I will always be there for him, and he will spend every summer with me. However, deep inside, I have this haunting feeling that life will never be the same for him. Life is strange! I have been trying to understand human nature for all these years. Maybe if we correspond, I will understand a little more, maybe not.

I am a computer scientist with two master's degrees. I am working in the software development field. I am very intelligent (how pompous that sounds!), but I know I am too smart for my own good. You see, my problem is that I am too curious. I cannot accept things at face value, especially things that are of human value. I like to be challenged mentally and, over the years, I have noticed that I have developed annoying habits that come, I suppose, with getting older. I have become very cynical. Already, I sense a tragic momentum so I am assuming that your life has been very challenging.

Do you have pictures of yourself? I would like to link the words to an image.

So you wrote the story of your life! Are the thirty-five chapters linked to each year of the past thirty-five years of your life? How will you write about the future? How will you write about the end? Maybe over time you will provide me with your work. So the floor is yours and I am all ears. Tell me more about yourself.

Bye.

February 4.

Simone,

The searing pain of emotional loss is something to be shared if, eventually, you can do so. Maybe through that sharing, I might begin to understand something of my own mother's feelings (if indeed there were any), through you.

The loss of my mother is, I suppose, fundamental to my being. To talk of this is, perhaps, a little premature, I think. As for who I am; who knows? I sense that nothing in me is ordinary. I fought my way to an education. I fought for my undergraduate education, my MBA, and my doctorate. Despite these successes, I have recently been struck by a melancholy. I had not thought of my mother in years. She disappeared from my mind – seemingly, unconsciously; it was the result of some mental defence mechanism. It was not until I had completed my MBA, in my late twenties, that I made a first effort to establish her whereabouts.

I suppose it was only at that moment that I felt worthy. It is nonsense, I know, but that is the whole point about emotional reasoning. It is, or can be, nonsensical. I seem to have her image in front of me – though indiscernible – almost daily. Whether through yearning or contempt, I have a need for her. Would the impact of her departure be of interest?

John.

February 6.

John,

Yes, I would like to know how the departure of your mother impacted your outlook on life. I am also open to hearing all the details of your own life as well. I hope to present you with understanding and be a good reader/listener. I will give you my input and perspective concerning the most sensitive details if you want to share any.

The beauty of this correspondence is that you do not have to pretend to be anything but yourself, right? Is that possible? Can you write all the sensitive details of your personal life in a book, I wonder? What is it that you have in your life that compelled you to write thirty-five years' worth of memories?

Tell me, John. Are you married? Do you have children? What is your life all about? Do you have a picture of yourself? I am open. I guess it is up to you to share, if you desire, your inner-most thoughts. I will be a confidant and will not compromise your trust.

Simone.

February 9.

Simone,

Pictures? I thought we were going to occupy a world of ideas? Let me succumb, partially. I am around six foot, angular in appearance and lean. I used to run. I still keep in shape at the gym.

As I mentioned earlier, I have had an ambition to write autobiographically for years but never had the opportunity until recently. The first chapter was the hardest. Just getting thoughts on paper and forcing my mind to re-enter the past was a struggle. Each chapter was successively easier to write. I wrote from a personal and innocent perspective. There is little salacious thought or description in the text – now three short volumes of fifteen chapters each. There is, though, the scene when I first became aware of my mother as an object of latent sensuality.

We were to be going somewhere or other. I was standing by the bed; I remember my waist being about the height of the mattress. I suppose I was around four. I watched her move from one place to another. She was wearing a raincoat. It was tied at her waist. I looked at the folds formed by the tightness of the belt. I was moved visually and felt something beyond the childlike love I had known up until that moment. Something else was going on. I became excited between my legs. Stiffness took hold. God (though I did not realise it at the time), I was having my first erotic experience and what better confirmation than to have a solid erection. After that, I had little awareness of her. I do not understand why.

In writing, I suppose the notion of structure appeals so I mapped out the general phases or themes for the first volume and simply started writing. What was I trying to convey? I suppose the struggle to survive, emotionally as well as materially. The underlying theme is that of being buffeted by forces that are beyond a mere mortal's control.

Are we going to be friends? Will we endure, do you think?

John.

February 9.

Dear John,

Yes, I would like to build a friendship with you. Your soul is very safe with me. I will not compromise you in any form. What

19

you write to me will be held in the utmost security. I want you to trust me and over time you will get to know me well. I am a very caring and warm person, or at least I have been told as much by many people. I will send you my picture. Whether you want to send me yours or not is up to you. I will be fine with whatever you decide. I think it is important for both of us to have an image of who we are in our minds as we correspond. My picture is in the office but I will send it tomorrow.

Simone.

At this point, John was a little concerned that reality was already creeping into the correspondence. This was not his intention at all. He wanted to retain the purity of thought, no matter where that might lead, as a journey of exploration. He did not want the confusion of a flesh-and-blood reality. If that had been his desire, he would have selected a potential reader of his thoughts from within the borders of his own country. What was he to do? He began to succumb to temptation. After all, she was still on the other side of the Atlantic!

February 10.

John,

Your very brief description of your features left out many details. What colour are your eyes and hair? I really would appreciate a picture. Who set the rules, by the way? Let us agree to one thing and I hope that you do not mind. Our communication should have no rules. Here is where the soul should have free domain to feel, express, and expand. You are on the verge of bearing your soul to me. I am very honoured and promise you that I shall be a loyal confidant. I will not disappear suddenly. I will respond to your your e-mails always unless I or one of the kids is sick. As for me, I am a petite woman. I am 5' 4", 120 lbs., with brown hair, brown eyes, and olive skin. I am of Spanish descent now living in New York City. You will see who I am tomorrow. I will only be separated from my son. My daughter, who is nine months old, will remain with me. I have been married for seven years. My husband and I have come to a point where we cannot communicate any more. We are almost always fighting. He tells me that I have changed! Marriage is quite an institution, but that is another lengthy conversation. We will discuss its details later. He will go to California and take my son with him. During school time, my child will be with him but during the summer months my son will stay with me. I cannot lose him.

I am so mortified that he will end up blaming me for letting him leave. I must do all I can to keep communicating with him. I will call and visit when he moves. He is my sunshine. I bathe him, shower him with kisses and he innocently tells me to not kiss him! He tells me that he is a big boy now and does not want me to kiss him, so I laugh and give him a big hug and kiss him even more. I tickle him and wrestle with him. He asks me a lot of questions about everything. He is bright and handsome, and I do not want the situation to harm him.

My husband and I sleep in separate rooms. My daughter sleeps in my bed with me and my son sleeps in the other room with his father. I come in, in the morning, after his father has already left for work, and slip into the bed and hug him and hold him so close to my heart. Sometimes I cry.

Sometimes I read a book to him. I brush his hair and tell him never to forget that I will always love him. He looks me and asks me why. My heart throbs with so much pain at his very innocence. Should I continue to be married and sacrifice my life and career for the sake of the children? I cannot. I am very tired and my marriage is such a disaster.

Well, I am really sorry that you do not have much memory of your mother. It is hard. Did someone else take care of you? Was there a motherly figure in your life? Was your father caring and loving? Did he hug you? Did he comfort you? How did you cope with the loss of your mother? Did you cry when you needed her and she was not there? Did you blame yourself? Did you miss her? Please, tell me!

I can only imagine how my son will react when he leaves me. I don't think he realizes what is about to happen to him.

Your comment about your erection with your mother is actually a real psychologically childish reaction. Was it a passing feeling or did you have any lingering feelings for a motherly figure in your life? Do you have erotic dreams and thoughts? How do you deal with women? Are you shy? What is it that is weighing on your soul so much at this stage of your life? Are you lonely? Do you wish to be warmly held and loved?

Simone.

3.

February 14.

Simone,

I read about the pending loss of your son and wondered, though only fleetingly, whether any such thoughts passed through the mind and heart of my mother. My memory of her is so fragmented. I seem to have cast her adrift, allowing her to descend into the deepest recesses of my mind and, I suppose, my heart. No motherly figure appeared to take her place. Five years later, I was at school in England. There was a temporary teacher. She was Austrian. I fell in love with her. I was only ten. For the two previous years, I was fixated by my two primary school teachers. One, Miss Purdie, wore strong colours; like deep red and dark green, both over black. I used to daydream about her. She had dark hair and was curvaceous, a sort of Jane Russell, even with the latter's almost sneering smile. The second was Miss Anderson, slight and blonde, who wore swirling dresses. As she taught, she would toss her ubiquitous piece of chalk repeatedly in the air. I was transfixed with this and her. I had dreams about her. My nakedness was included in some. The Austrian woman, though, was of a different type. Using film actresses again, she was like a Heddy Lamar (no wonder Victor Mature's Samson got caught out). I was very sad when she left. No such potentially maternal figures appeared again at school.

You asked if someone else, a "motherly figure", appeared in my life. A second mother did appear. I never used a parental endearment with her; I always called her by her first name. I did so unconsciously and only realized the significance in my twenties. 'Was your father caring and loving with you? Did he hug you? Did he comfort you?' I suppose he cared about me in his way but I will write about that another time.

You want to know how I coped with losing my mother. That is the thing. She disappeared from my thoughts, my mind, my memory and even, it appears, my heart. It is something I simply cannot explain. I hinted previously that it must have been some sort of automatic defence mechanism taking hold. I suppose Freud would have a good understanding and subsequent explanation. I am no Freud.

You indicated that you are worried about your son's reaction to losing you. That is the awfulness of the situation. You want him to maintain that love for you but, in doing so, he shall feel pain again and again as he wakes up knowing that you are not in the next room. Yet, in order to grow into a whole and caring human being, this is a pain that he must absorb.

As for your inquiry about the sexual memory I have of my mother, I can tell you that, apart from my teachers, most of my fantasies have been about being bathed by a woman – an innocent delusion. I suppose I have other erotic thoughts like any other person but have never tried to express them until this moment. I was painfully shy when younger but I have grown out of that.

Now I dream of little but abandoned reality, the layers of consciousness laid bare upon the floor, allowing me to step away and drift to warm water and caring hands. There is a rapidly growing awareness that I inhabit two worlds: one of day-to-day realities and the other of the mind. The latter must ultimately be invigorated in order keep the daily world workable. Yet those realities must not be compromised otherwise everything collapses. The edifice must stand despite itself. You are very sympathetic and, it seems, very understanding.

John.

February 15.

Simone,

Let me illustrate my early shyness and confusion with a woman. As a teenager, I was supremely fit, strong and fast. My school combined team games with fitness training, through endurance running. Even if someone failed academically (some did and I was one of them), at least they would have a fit and healthy body from all that physical exertion. The point of telling you this is to set the scene for my first (and some would say *distorted*) encounter. It is captured in my early autobiographical writing.

'Meanwhile, Judy, my stepmother, was getting herself set for her departure as well. They agreed that she would leave the day John did. That night John's father was not around. He was away on another binge. Judy told John to sleep his father's bed; there were two single beds. He did. He purposely did not hide himself while taking his clothes off. His erection was pulsating. He crept into bed. He lay awake for ages, shaking, wondering if any hint would be offered. He yearned, and then ached for it. He wanted to climb in with her. She didn't say anything. John didn't say anything, and John didn't move. He fell asleep, alone. That was the last time they were in a bedroom together.

John.'

February 16.

John,

Attached you will find my pictures and that is the closest thing you will get to my physical reality. I think it would help both of us to know the physical vessels which contain our spirits. I attach a picture of my son as well.

I suppose I am basically blocking all my vulnerability and weakness of heart at this point, even though deep inside, I know if I were to face what is happening and the inevitable separation from my child, I will surely not be able to deal with it. I am not sure if this is courage or escape. If courage, then you seem to be introducing me to the concept. If escape, then it is certainly a pleasant one for the moments that I enter this new world of ours. I will not compromise your reality. I actually thought to myself that is a really interesting statement as I have always struggled to maintain a sense of reality. My day-to-day life is so disconnected from my internal thoughts and beliefs, and how I view the world.

I dared to share my thoughts and my views on life with my husband. He could not handle it of course! This is part of the reason we are divorcing. I felt betrayed when I opened my soul to him. Of course, I should have known better. He did nothing. He said nothing. In essence he just closed me off and walked away. I so desperately wanted him. I wanted to walk with him and talk with him. He would have none of it. It was as if he had transformed himself or had been transformed by some force external to himself. Whatever the reason, the end was embedded in that moment.

I would love to get a close-up picture of you so I can see your face and eyes. Is this possible? I hope that I am not overly bold in demanding such reality but it is only for a simple reason. I just need to have an image of you when I discuss very sensitive things. I do not understand why I have this need.

I am very focused and have pursued a path of self-preservation as well through my life. Therefore, it has always been critical for me to excel and always achieve in the corporate world of business. I learned over time to become realistic about life. I was such an idealist; so naive and so trusting.

I did not get any serious details regarding your virginity experience. I am not sure if that is the way you meant it. Did you end up making love to your step-mother or did you end up masturbating? I am sorry to ask a blunt question but what I think would help you is to talk about this experience at length, not just the physical aspect of it as much as your feelings before, during and after. It seems that you were left with emptiness and confusion.

As for me, let me share my virginity story with you. I was eighteen and it was the first year in college. I was madly in love with him. He was older, he was inspiring, he was handsome and he seemed to exude a spirituality, something I was only becoming aware of from different sources of writing. I did not really plan or think that it would happen. He and I sat on the top of the college roof. We were kissing softly and looking deeply into each other's eyes. He embraced me so strongly I thought I would not be able to breathe. He started to unbutton my blouse and I was overcome by my feelings. It did not hurt and I did not bleed, and that, my friend, turned into a big problem afterwards. He doubted my virginity and that was the beginning of the end of my first love. I will tell you much more later.

Yesterday, I had a very strange thought of you. I thought that you are still a child, the same four-year-old child standing in the room with his mother you described to me in your earlier message. Here I am with the same situation with my son. My son is leaving me but the energy of the universe brings me your spirit, the spirit of a four-year-old child yearning for his mother. I cried. I thought maybe the universe is giving you, through me, a chance to reach into the past and touch that very moment of your separation from your mother. Maybe the energy or spirit of your mother is localised in some form in me. I do not know. I hope that this does not scare you away, but I want to be honest with you. Maybe the wisdom of it all is that I will be the key to releasing your emotions. This is really so strange and potentially wonderful. What do you think?

Simone.

February 18.

Simone,

You said you did not get enough details from me regarding my virginity experience. I neither slept with my stepmother nor masturbated and that is the tragedy of a lost moment. So, let me test this new world of ours and imagine how it *might* have been, should have been and, oh, how I deeply wanted it to be. Recently, I decided to write about that scene, possibly to see if I should include it in some of my autobiographical writing.

'I am almost eighteen and look upon her. My stomach muscles are quivering, literally. She is not feeling very well and had another furious row with my father. He has left and won't be back. I move to her. She has tears in her eyes and wipes them away. She can see that I am nervous and, after a moment, realises that I am aching for release. She looks at me and shows understanding. She sits up in bed and asks me to sit beside her. Quivering has moved to shaking. She places her hand on my lap. "You cannot do this to me; we cannot sleep together," she says but with nothing but care and sympathy. She asks, "Have you slept with a girl?"

'I shake my head. She looks at me again and takes my hand. She places it softly on her breast. I pull back sharply, fearing the beauty and softness of it and the contradiction of rejection.

She takes my hand again. "Let me help you just a little." She places it in the warmth of her breast again. I swallow deeply and linger. I feel the hardening of her nipple. My heart is racing. She looks at me and puts her hand on my lap. She sees the bulging evidence of my need for her. She understands. She moves her hand inside my jeans. I shudder. She knows I must be freed from this tension. She is still sitting in bed, smiling gently. She is a woman I have never really known and yet, on this night, just before she leaves her husband forever, she reaches out to me with tenderness and a smile of insight at my youthful dilemma.

'She asks me if I am afraid, and I tell her I am. She takes off my jeans and I take off my shirt. I am left with only my boxer shorts. I stand and she pulls them down. She takes a sudden breath, looking in admiration. I am in peak physical condition. My manhood is large and very erect to the point of discomfort; the blood pressure is so intense that things must start quickly. I become a little more assertive. "Now?" I ask her.

'She takes me in her hand to start me off, then lies back and watches, stretching out a hand to caress my balls, to heighten my pleasure. "Is it nice?" I ask. "Please tell me it's nice!"

'"Yes, it's very nice!" she replies.

'"Is it beautiful; is it really beautiful; please tell me, please?" As I plead and as she offers reassurance, my body, already firm, starts to arch with thrilling spasms. My arms, my chest, my stomach and thighs are all rigid with the anticipation of total release. My jaw is clenched tightly as my hand moves faster and with greater intensity. I feel the magic start, moving from the depths of my secret parts. It rushes through ("I'm coming, aahhhhhhh") then spurts out through the tip of my cock. She has already cupped her hands to catch the lovely fluid (to stop it getting on to the bed sheets). I fall to my knees on the edge of the bed but remain upright. My body glistens with the pink colouring of effort.

"Are you all right?"

I nod shyly.

"Good, then go and get a cloth and towel to clear this up."

'I do and, with a warm cloth, wipe her hands clean. She takes me gently in her hand and makes sure any residue is removed from my masculinity. I pull my boxers on and sit a moment. She holds my hand and looks at me, kisses my cheek, then says, "Go to bed now, John. One day, you will find real happiness."

'For that moment, we are innocently as one. For that moment, I think I feel loved.'

You transcend time and space. How have we connected? Are you my mother reincarnated, at least in spirit? What is this? Are you the mirror for my mother's pain; am I the mirror for your sson's? Are we to seek mutual understanding and eventual healing through this?

Even through your pain, you feel so strong! I could drown in your strength. I could abandon life and sink into your arms. Maybe that would let me open the caverns where the emotions attempt to reconcile themselves. Maybe the interminable process of reconciliation has gone stale. The struggle has grown weary and confused, where real life has been reduced to the mechanical and the routine. You are new spirit, a beguiling reawakening. If we are to flourish in this secret world of ours, there should be absolutely no censorship at all. Agreed?

John.

4.

February 21.

Dear John,

Your ability to write, even in imagination, about such an emotionally explosive experience tells me that you are no ordinary mortal. Words such as yours are a gift; have you ever thought about writing professionally? I am so curious about you. What kind of man are you? What lies dormant in that imagination of yours? Let's see. Maybe not today or tomorrow but, let's see, eventually. This is exciting!

Now, let us move on to calmer things. Let me tell you a little about my background. I was born the fourth child of five, into a very loving family. My mother and father married for love. Still, today, they are like lovebirds, caring about each other. I come from a big family of two uncles and more cousins. As a child, I was very precocious. I learned to read and write earlier than my peers. My mother and father had a difficult time when young. My mother is Catalonian and my father is a Basque. When he decided to marry her, of course, many relatives objected. However, my father insisted. My mother was introduced to our family at an early age, seventeen. She was so beautiful. She suffered a lot of prejudice. She was an orphan who lost her mother and father at the age of two. Her grandmother raised her but she suffered tremendously because she had no emotional care. Her grandmother was a cold lady. Therefore, my mother is very affectionate and tried to make up all the love she never had by mothering us. She was very demanding of our excellence in school, manners and good behaviour. She felt that she had to prove to my father's family that we are the best of our kind. It was good and bad. It was good that her children were the smartest and most mannered. It was bad as many jealousies and conflicts occurred between us and our cousins.

I re-read your 'youthful experience' e-mail. You strike me as a very sensitive man. Your words are so simple, yet very powerful. Of course, I agree with you. Neither one of us should censor this relationship. I find a lot of comfort when confiding in you. I need to do so as much as you do. I did not expect our correspondence to take such a turn. My intent was to review your writing and provide you with my input. However, from the first e-mail that you sent, I felt that there was a divine purpose in our communication. The connection of your childhood and my situation is profound. I am sure in time we will learn much about the randomness of fate and what is in store for both of us.

Well, I will give you a backdrop to my early years and my first love so that you will understand the ramifications of that situation. In conventional rural Catholic communities, a woman's honour is directly linked to her virginity. I was very much in love and more than a little rebellious back then. My lover was a liberal academic. I was very taken by his words and passion for fighting for a better society with freedom and democracy for all. It was so compelling to see him address crowds of students with speeches about the future and the ills of our society. Of course, part of the liberation was that of pursuing sexual freedom for women. I liked the idea. I believed in him. I was not active in politics like he was but admired and supported him.

After we made love and I showed no signs of virginity, he was very upset. This was contrary to his beliefs and speeches. He treated me just like an ignorant Catholic traditionalist. He was so consumed with anger over doubting that he was not the first man in my life. He *was* the first man in my life and I was so upset to face his hypocrisy and lies. I saw the truth of the ideas he promoted in his speeches but, under the veneer of liberation, he had a very closed mind. I saw that his political activities were nothing but a means to become someone important in the scheme of the student body.

He started to abuse me. He thought he owned me. He viewed me now as something he could simply use as opposed to love. That was how it came across to me. He started making love with an additional intensity. The former tenderness was gone. In its place was something I later realised was domination. He made me lean forward against a chest of drawers for example. I was scared. I let him. He entered me harshly and found his way to his own pleasure. It was confusing because it started to stir things within me that I did not understand at the time. He used this technique a few times. Once I came with such power, my knees buckled! The point though was that he thought he owned me by mere virtue of thinking that I was not a virgin. He told me that no other man would touch me. I found later that he was involved with another woman. Little did he know that I had a fighting spirit. I asked to end the relationship. He was shocked and could not believe that I would dare to let him go.

I want to stop here. It bothers me to have these memories come back and haunt me. The most painful part is the loss of innocence to the reality of people and life. Many things have happened and I will share more with you.

Simone.

February 22.

Dear Simone,

You hint at the erotic and have even asked me to share such thoughts with you. I have genuinely rejoiced in that release. Perhaps one day, you will reciprocate.

In the movie *Zorba the Greek,* Alan Bates asked Anthony Quinn, "Are you married?"

Quinn responded, "Yes! House, wife, children; the full catastrophe!"

My wife, Heather, is athletic in frame from a passion for swimming from an almost unhealthily young age. She was an English Olympic hopeful. At one point, like you, she rebelled from the convention of having to achieve in ways that others determined. She walked out of the whole thing to devote her time to serious university studies. She got a very good degree, in English, and went into literary publishing. It is almost ironic that I now inhabit this surreal world, sharing sensitive, intimate and even erotic thoughts with you.

We have three children. The last was quickly diagnosed as having Down's syndrome. From that moment on, her spirit ebbed visibly from her mind and her body. Her courageous decision to abandon competitive swimming in order to pursue an intellectual and, finally, a domestic life, was thrown in her face. The other two children are fine.

The realisation of having a seriously disabled child hit me like a sledgehammer. It's as if we have been punished for a crime we have not committed. In any event, our family now proceeds with life more mechanically than emotionally. I love my children dearly and spend as much time with them as I can, but I travel a lot.

I'm in the telecommunications industry and I am often away to all parts of Britain and sometimes overseas. The international dimension seems an increasing prospect. I find the possibility of working in India particularly interesting. I know Britain is a small country but, with regional offices scattered all over, there is a lot of work.

I have never strayed in the sense of the carnal knowledge of another person. Yet, as I travel around and see the variations in the struggle to live, let alone survive, I wonder if this is all there is to life. My mind works hard and yet I know it has so much unused potential. It was this realisation and the certainty that I was being totally consumed by the conventional and the mechanical that was beginning to disturb me.

At first, anger was the order of the day. That anger transformed into an initial, then deepening, depression. I could have gone to the doctor. He would have prescribed some pill or other. I might have been offered group therapy. Neither would have been acceptable. I had come this far, virtually alone. I was going to get through it one way or the other. Hence, I sent out a cry for help to one old friend, then another. The rest, as they say, is history, for you appeared from nowhere, as if sent from heaven. There is a subversive reality in the universe. I suppose porn is one manifestation, though I have not ventured down that path, yet. What I find stunning is the thought that I have such potential thoughts and the capacity for thinking in such ways. I need a friend to explore them with me and, given that we are on opposite sides of the Atlantic, it remains a safely abstract notion, comforting yet vicariously exciting. I take great pleasure in your revelations and I think, you in mine. You may wonder why I do not share such things with Heather.

Her life is now full-to-overflowing with the reality and additionally tragic challenges of life, emotionally as well as practically. To burden her (and I know it would be so after twenty years) would be to kill what we have left. I must, therefore, nourish that other side of me elsewhere in order to retain my strength and vigour. Then I can honour the survival of my family. I suppose at the end of all this is a feeling of emptiness; the loneliness of a motherless boy now compounded by the realities of an adulthood, where the strength of a woman he married and loves has been shattered and where life, in its need to continue, yearns for that ultimate maternal protection. Does that make sense? These are ideas I need to explore.

John.

February 25.

John,

I'm so sorry. Tragedy hits so many people: you with Andrew and the devastation of your wife. Me with the mess I am in now! Let's just take this journey together and see where it goes. Okay?

I thought of you last night. My husband and I went to the movies and watched *Gladiator*. It was a very good story. I love the Roman era and the plot was very moving. This morning is rainy and quiet. I put on *Moonlight Sonata*. I listen to this often as it fills my heart with emotions. It is so hauntingly sad.

I rush my responses to you. I hope I am not stressing you with having to respond. Take your time. Savour my thoughts and tell me what you feel and what you think. I am enjoying our correspondence tremendously. I have thought about our connection. I rarely do venture to discuss such intimate details of my life with anyone. I actually do not like to do so but you are an exception. I can tell from the way you write that you are an exceptional person whom I need to talk to. I believe in the mechanics of some form of universal energy that is watching over us. There is a reason and we shall find it as we communicate more.

I am not psychic nor do I claim to have any special powers but I am very sensitive to the paranormal. I can feel many things and have been trying, through meditation and a lot of exploration of myths, religion, history and people, to understand what this life and universe is all about. Let tell you about the thoughts I had last night.

I thought about your childhood. I thought of your mother and tried to channel her spirit. I tried to feel if it is really her spirit that is behind our communication. I closed my eyes and slowed my breathing until I achieved a meditative state. I saw a woman in the woods. In such states, I do not see clear images as much as I feel the surroundings. It was very, very cold. She was so very sad and stunningly beautiful. She had long, black curly hair, and on her feet she wore leather sandals. The sandals might have been deer leather; they wrapped around her legs up to the knees. She had on a heavy coat made of animal skin, which covered her from head to toe. It had no sleeves but rather, it draped around her shoulders like a blanket. I felt her sharp and incredibly deep sadness. There was snow and a light chilling wind. Her eyes gazed into the distance. She was thinking. She had a pack of wolves by her. I thought to myself that is strange. Are they wolves or are they dogs? I could not tell. They felt her pain too. I heard the sound of a fast object piercing the air. It was an arrow that suddenly made a thud as it found its target. I looked in shock and saw that it hit her. I saw her blood darken the snow. She did not panic or cry. She extended her hand in the air as she fell to the ground and the wolves howled in sadness. The image faded, and I left my trance.

I do not yet fully understand these visions.

Now, you must think that I am totally crazy. I am not. I opened myself a long time ago to the energy of the universe to try and understand who I am. I think that I understand the dynamics of our communication. I am not saying that the energy of your mother is trying to reach you. No, I do not think so but maybe it is. I am not sure. I thought early this morning that through me, you will be there for my grief as I lose my child. You will understand the love of a grieving mother. Maybe that is the gift of the universe to you at this point in your life. I am not sure but that is what I feel.

Do I have erotic thoughts? Yes! I will describe my thoughts on making love to a man. I dream of my lover touching me in the stillness of the moment and gazing into my eyes. He embraces me so very softly and feels my loving warmth as I wrap my arms around him. As we hold on to each other, we breathe together. I feel protected and cherished as he buries his nose in my hair and smells the sweetness of my perfume. I brush his hair gently with the tips of my fingers and whisper in his ear words of my love and affection. To me it is the feeling of complete unity and trust that makes my heart throb, not the mechanics of the physical act, although I do too enjoy the physical sensation. It is magical only when I am in love.

I will describe more of my thoughts later to you but will stop here for now. At this point, I wonder what you think of me! I am smiling now. Yes, I am surprised! We did come a long way in such a short time. I will wait to hear more from you.

Simone.

5.

February 27.

Dear Simone,

You make me shake with excitement at your mysterious visions. I do not understand them, nor have I any experience at believing such things. The excitement is of knowing someone who can be consumed by such mysteries. That, on its own, strikes me as being a deeply, even darkly, erotic quality. What am I saying here for heaven's sake? Such an idea has never entered my head, let alone crossed my lips. You have a kind of energy, the like of which I have never experienced before. It is beguiling and sensuous. I wonder what is going on between us. You are a revelation, an object of love and, almost, adoration. Your descriptions of making love in a sea of emotion are sublime. I know no such feelings or heights of potential ecstasy. I suppose I am emotionally barren. Yes, I make love at times, though I confess that, for me, it is the mechanics that dominate the process – though I would elevate that word to technique. To make love with emotion, surely one has to have an emotional foundation. Without that foundation, it is not possible to break through and be a complete being in that totally loving sense. I love my wife and children. My wife is my best friend but that friendship involves all things related to our family. I don't think I can conceive of the way you describe acts of intimacy. It is simply beyond me. Is that an awful thing to say?

Again, there are times, even in these middle adult years, when I revert automatically to something much younger. I see or hear a strong woman and my heart yearns to be consumed by that strength so I can be taken away from reality. Such strength would allow me, in her presence, to divest myself of the trappings of life and allow the emotional healing process – or building from scratch – to take hold. I fear to write more lest you think badly of me, and yet I long for complete abandon and emotional completeness without reproach, with a complete absence of judgment.

The mechanics of reality and survival can be a lonely business.

John.

February 27.

John,

I have been thinking about your last e-mail. Let us talk at length about your loneliness. What drives such feelings? I am sure that you love your children and wife but where is the vacuum? You need a "strong" woman. What makes a woman strong in your mind? Let me hear more from you. Tell me how you feel about women sexually and emotionally. Have you ever been in love? Do you feel loved? I am here for you.

Simone.

February 28.

Simone,

I have diligence in operational love; it is a love of safety, comfort and protection of and for my family and their survival and development. Andrew raises that to a different dimension, with his mental and emotional confinement. Do I feel loved? Yes, conventionally, but in terms of succour and true abandon? No. That is elusive and seems destined to remain so. I hope that with this emotional candour and personal intimate information I have written about, you have not been offended or even shocked into mere politeness. We did agree earlier – no censorship!

John.

March 2.

John,

I am so glad you were able to write to me! I do not want to censor anything in our communication, and I do not mind sharing the most intimate of details between us. You are not offending me in any way. Actually, you write so nicely and so gently. In time, we will share a deeper level of openness in describing details of intimacy. It is important to feel no inhibition and to exercise a wide measure of trust and openness.

My moments of privacy are very few these days as my mother and father are visiting us. They visit once every year and end up staying for a month or so. My husband and I decided not to tell them that we are separating in August.

We explained the fact that we sleep in different rooms because of my nine-month-old baby. She wakes up frequently during the night and I need to take care of her.

Let me see. Last time I ended my story at the point where my first love ended. I do not have much time for privacy now. I will send you more details later.

I wanted to tell you that I am so thrilled to be able to talk to you. It is so uplifting to have this freedom to share my thoughts and feelings so openly.

I look forward to seeing your picture soon!

Meanwhile, I have to fix dinner and will give you more details about what happened next in my life after I ended my relationship. At the time, I thought that my life was over. I had no reason to continue living as I was so shattered by his betrayal. Little did I know what was in store for me. More details later.

I'm in the mood to write, so I will now bombard you with my thoughts; please, excuse me. It seems to be helping to put my current troubles into a little perspective, so, let me continue with my story.

In the course of three months after my first experience with my lover, we came to an abrupt end. I chose to end the relationship as he was treating me very abusively. I have already mentioned about the dominating aspect of things. My problem was that I could feel a contradiction emerging within me. I knew what he was doing was something that I should not tolerate and yet for a time, I did. It was physical. It was sensual. For some reason, inexplicable, it was exciting. It was as if some darkness was being tapped within me. I have no idea if such potential lies within all of us, yet it was there. I had to wrestle with myself. He was so sure of himself that I had no choice. I was in a very bad situation. However, I did not care. I was fed up with his hypocrisy. Finally, I broke free. That was indeed literal as well as emotional.

The literal concerned yet one more time where I was pushed against a wall so that he could start yet another round of his conquest. Finally, I felt my mind snapping with anger. I was dazed for a few weeks thereafter. I was in total shock. I couldn't believe how I let myself be treated in such a way. Yet I also couldn't believe the recognition of something dormant within me.

It took me three years before I met my husband. I told myself back then that I do not need men and decided to not pursue marriage. I did not want to have to deal with another man's narrow-minded attitude and incriminations. I just promised myself to excel academically and focus on a very bright career. However, the adverse outcome was that I turned from a very dynamic outgoing person to an introvert. I did not interact with any of my male colleagues and luckily my ex-love decided to drop the computer school and move to the law school. That was great so I did not have to see him at all. The three years passed so fast and in these years I turned to books. I read and read and read. I lived among books and my activities were restricted from school to my parent's house. I never dwelt on it or looked back. I had this enormous inner strength: whatever it is that I have to face in life, my education and career will protect me. I planned to become financially independent.

Three years later, a friend of mine asked me for a favour. She told me that there was an American guy who was visiting school who needed an interpreter; he knew no Spanish. I was known to have the best command of English in our school. I agreed, reluctantly. The reason for my reluctance was this friend was a political activist. I knew that the conversations would be political and I had no interest. I interpreted for the group and everyone was happy. I went about my business and all of them left as well. As I was leaving the building, my future husband was there chatting with someone who was in the group so I smiled as I was passing them. He asked me if I would give him a tour of the campus. I was taken aback. I agreed and we walked around and we talked a little. He was so thoughtful and I really enjoyed his company. I ended up walking him around for two hours. He asked me if he could see me again. I agreed. I will let you know more. I have to stop now. I have yet to get your picture as well!

Simone.

March 5.

Simone,

My unfolding story is one of a boy's struggle to get through high school.

I excelled at sports. I was less successful in my academic courses. Because of this, my chances of getting into college were slim. There was only one thing I could think of. I have always been keen on boats (for some inexplicable reason, or maybe not – more on that in a moment). The navy had a smart uniform and a good reputation for training its people in skills that would be useful in later life. I thought that it would be practical choice. I started making discreet inquiries. In my late teens, I took an aptitude test and discovered that parts of my brain were actually working to the point of impressing the people who tested me. I wanted to be an electrical technician, good practical work where problems would be encountered, and I would jump in and solve them. With the aptitude test behind me, that only left the medical examination. At that time, I was taller than most and certainly faster. I played rugby in winter and flew up and down the wing. Someone once suggested that I should become a county player at least and go on from there. I had no interest. I revelled in the ability to run (and tackle) at speed but it was the speed that attracted me to the sport, not the competitive aspect itself. I never pushed it. What I did push was the navy.

When the news broke at home, there was an unholy row. Tempers erupted and, for the first time in my life, I discovered that I had a temper of my own. That night, the cord with my father was finally severed. He had delusions of me entering college; the delusion was to carry kudos for him with his friends and colleagues. He wanted to hold his head up with his peers so that he could talk of his son 'at university'. The scene was a brutal one. He wanted to take me into the yard and 'beat the shit' out of me. I knew that if it came to it, I would inflict immense physical damage on him; I was two inches taller, didn't smoke, didn't drink and had the fitness of a serious athlete.

Everything I was, he was not. My completely uncharacteristic temper surged and as it did, I realised what was about to happen. I could have killed him. Rational thought managed to invade my mind. The relationship died at that moment and my tears came with it. How I howled in anguish as I ran. I ran and ran and ran until I reached my girlfriend's home, two miles away.

When I recovered, I vowed that I would make my own decisions and make my own mistakes in life.

By then the papers were already safely through, and I was off to Portsmouth to start my naval training. Not much of a story there except to confirm a virginal innocence generally and with the gentler sex particularly. My girlfriend was just that. We kissed often and fondled occasionally but nothing was consummated.

My girlfriend lived with her grandmother. I slept there that night, recovering from the tears I had shed on arrival. The following day, I went back to my parent's apartment, where I found the few things that belonged to me. It was all so easily packed into one suitcase. I took it to the station; it was being sent to my former teacher for safekeeping. My girlfriend met me at the apartment. It was time to close that episode completely. We walked back towards the station. My father was approaching. We came together. I continued to walk, offering an almost inaudible "Hello".

I never saw my father again and the purpose of having a stepmother vanished. I suppose if I knew then what I know now, it might have been different. I used to watch mothers with their sons and wonder what it must be like simply to be taken care of in that totality of innocence. I wondered what it would be like to be bathed by a mother (though by now, a mother figure!). I wondered if she would take me gently and caress me in the bath then cover me in warmth as well as water, then ask me to stand and glisten in front of her and then for her...

Well, let's just leave that for now. Nothing of the kind ever happened. The earlier imagined masturbation encounter was a similar fiction, as you know. What my mind was telling me (and my hardened manhood told me so) was that I wanted her but I simply couldn't unscramble my chaotic thinking. I just felt it. Anyway, everything came to an abrupt end.

In old fashioned parlance, I 'ran away' – from everything – and, for better or worse, never chose to look back, just like you, I suppose. It was a time of hope and exploration. In essence, I had been poverty-stricken. I had no money of my own to that point, being entirely dependent on my father. Entering the navy saw me with my first payment, a sort of 'signing-on' fee. I had never had money that wasn't to be spent for something in particular. It was such a release, a liberation even. Arriving in Portsmouth was like entering a world of uniformed comfort and care. Clothes were supplied, food was freely available, each day was packed with things to be done, things to be learnt and things to prepare for the next day. It was not only an antidote to emotional drama, it was the best form of reconstruction possible. I felt part of something. I felt important. I felt pride.

John.

March 6.

John,

I am going to a meeting in half an hour so I will type really fast. Well, I liked your e-mail but your missing details were revealing. It must be painful for you to not have communication with your family. I know that it was your own decision to cut off the link and move on with your life, but the yearning for a motherly touch is so powerful and to not have that is hard. My understanding is that, unfortunately, you did not have such emotional support from either parent. I am sure that you are more than compensating the loss of such support with your own children. You must be a very caring and loving father.

As I mentioned previously, my mother and father are visiting me. My mother will stay for four months but my father is leaving on June 22. He does not like to visit for long. I am very close to my father and in the past was Daddy's girl. I loved to impress him with my grades and academic excellence. I always undertook competitions and dared to win just to see his pride. It meant so much to me.

My mother was barely able to keep her head straight while taking care of her five children. She is very, very loving, and she was very tough on us in demanding excellence in every way. She had great concern for being proper and having manners. I remember that she took extra care to make sure that we are very well behaved children. However, with my father we had a more relaxed relationship. My father had to work two jobs to support us. Life was not harsh financially but it was not comfortable either. We learned to share with siblings. We never thought of ourselves as wanting in any way. my father came home from his work, we would all crowd around him and hug him and kiss him as it would be not until eight or nine in the evening that he would arrive. He managed to send all of us to university and gave us the best education. I will follow up with another e-mail for more details on my marriage.

Simone.

6.

March 7.

Dear John,

Another burst of writing from me. Please just let it wash over you, absorbing it at your own pace.

Let me write a little bit about love from the emotional side. To me, love is rapture. It is one of those bonds that are so strange in the way they develop and so painful in the way they die. I have fallen deeply in love twice. The first experience was so intense. I would feel extreme measures of emotion like happiness, sadness, longing, and desire for complete union emotionally and physically. It is really total surrender in trusting the beloved. I know that when I am in love, the sexual aspect is only an extension of my emotions. What is more rewarding and comforting are not the sexual aspects but the holding of hands, walking together, holding each other, talking to each other, looking into each other's eyes and breathing together while embracing. The senses of smell, touch, hearing and tasting, are very sharp and bring so much more joy to my heart. I do enjoy the sexual aspect too but the overwhelming factor for me is emotional. In a perfect relationship, these two are strongly intertwined. The sexual aspect to me is sacred in the sense that I am surrendering myself in the most intimate of ways. It is such a precious expression that I do not take lightly.

I know other people who do engage in sexual relationships for the physical gratification. I think that they are missing a lot and must feel the emotional vacuum usually after sex. Why? I believe it is because the experience is not complete. It is like the body and soul. You cannot really have life without both of them present at the same time.

Getting back to my story: I soon started meeting my husband in secret. He had a nice apartment, and I would sometimes skip half of a day of school and go to his place. The first time I visited him in his house was so emotional. He walked me through his apartment and we held hands as we did. We talked and talked about his life and mine. I was in heaven.

When we were in the study room, he reached and hugged me. I was almost breathless. I looked at him and he smiled as our lips touched. I thought that time stood still. That was all we did that day. We snuggled on the couch and held hands and talked for over three hours. It was magical.

The next time I visited him, we talked, kissed, and hugged. I trusted him and all my fears, years of isolation and mistrust evaporated. The first time we made love it was wonderful. I almost cried. I was so happy. He asked me to marry him. I could think of nothing more wonderful! It's difficult to explain why I was so much in belief of his love. They say that "love is blind". I would not argue with such a contention. I just knew that this was the man for me.

During that year I saw him every Saturday and our love grew stronger and stronger. I was not exposed to oral lovemaking at all. Actually, I did not know that there were so many variations and ways for making love.

One day, we were in the apartment and, as he was kissing me, he went down to my chest, then further, to my belly. He started to kiss and lick my belly in circular motion. I froze as I did not know what to do, but as he kept on kissing, I relaxed. He was on his knees and I was sitting on a very comfortable chair. I hugged his head as it lay in my lap. He then parted my legs and went down a little further to my feminine area; he very gently licked and kissed me there. As I felt waves of pleasure overtaking my body, he spread my legs further and sucked on me stronger. My body was shaking. I just thought I would explode with desire. I came with an intensity that I had never felt before. I was shaking for a few moments, so he held me and we kissed deeply.

This is one of the very special memories that I have and it was my first encounter with oral love. He had many other things to teach me. I soon discovered that my first encounter with so- called lovemaking with my ex-lover was really nothing compared to how I felt with my future husband. The memories of past pain evaporated, and I had full trust in my new love. Our love grew each time we met and we had this feeling of hope and happiness that was so magical. I knew in my heart that I would give him the world if he asked. I was so much in love with him.

Now, I still love my husband very dearly but I do not think that we are *in* love any more. Why does that happen?

It is so unfair.

Simone.

March 8.

Dear Simone,

As life unfolds I begin to wonder about the emotional strictures that confine most to a convention of love, let alone marriage. What you describe seems to have been the epitome of what love can be, but your question about why it does not last is an important one. I do not have an answer for you.

You describe your first oral encounter with such vividness and power – your shaking, the spasms of post-orgasmic pleasure. You also suggest that you have friends that delve into the idea of partners just for the physical gratification as though the sexual encounter is the ultimate itself, despite being divorced from a wider emotional rapture.

I confess to having sympathy with these people. I am not sure I have ever experienced that emotional rapture. I suppose, unwittingly perhaps, I pursued and eventually fell in love with someone with whom I emotionally bonded after the sexual frenzy subsided. Yet that did nothing to diminish the emotional love. It simply became my emotional reality. That is, emotion is separate from sex. I suppose Freud would have a field day with me for such a declaration. Does that explain my loneliness? Does that explain why I discovered "Personals" and then found you?

You have persisted with your request so try this FULL FRONTAL picture, I dare you!

John.

March 10.

John,

I was scared to open the attachment. I thought you had taken leave of your senses. I waited a day before doing so, thinking that you would not be so crazy as to pose naked for all to see.

What a picture! My god you are a good looking man! I had some vague notion in my head but frankly nothing like this. Your face is etched with experience. Those cheekbones make you look anything but English. The blond hair confirms it! I'm stunned.

Bye.

In fact, her reaction was nothing compared to her picture sent to him earlier. Online, one suspects whether the exquisite words, phrases and ideas will be matched by the visual reality. In Simone's case, it was most definitely so. She was olive in complexion, her hair was dark, her shape being quietly voluptuous. It was a stunning reality.

March 12.

Simone!

Stunned? I never reacted to your picture, because it was much earlier in our apparent timeless time together. As the image appeared, painfully slowly on to my screen, my breath was taken by such Latin loveliness. Those piercing – at one moment maternal and at another, deeply sensual – generating reactions in part of me that simply should not be and all based on a picture! But it is the picture and the intelligence behind it that is so thrilling.

Forgive me but in my less guarded moment, I would love to caress you intimately, but then, this is one of my rare unguarded moments!

John.

March 12.

John,

What did I tell you? No censorship! We should only have a free flow of thoughts and dreams. Dream of me, my friend. I am touched!

I am not feeling well today. I have to attend all-day meetings off-site. At home, I have my mother and father and family, so there is no privacy in which I can write. If I am late responding, it is only because I am trapped, with very little time. I am going through a very hard emotional time and this is really strange. Tell me a little about your feelings now. Why do you think that you are lonely? Give me more details. I am feeling very sad today. I have not felt this sad in a long time. I do not have time to write or explain but in time I will tell you. I will go home now. It will be three days or so before I can write you back. Please do not worry.

Simone.

March 13.

Simone,

My loneliness is hard to describe. The result I know only too well. Marriage is supposed to satisfy all things from the moment the bond is made until death takes one or both partner from this place. There seems to be something fanciful in that. Why do virile men, who are contentedly – let alone happily – married, seek further conquests of a physical kind? Why do increasing numbers of women divest themselves of the "gentler sex" veil and initiate similar activities. Why does this happen, though the perpetrators want to stay in the same marriage? For some it is genuine love, separate from rampant sexual desires. For others, it is economic reality – for women, economic dependency. For men, it is cheaper to stay together than to separate. Some stay together 'for the sake of the children'. For me, the issue is deeper.

I dare not burden Heather with more than she already has to contend at work, at home, and, especially, with the children. I tried to talk a few times but saw her exhaustion, already etched on her face, almost erupting into something worse. I quickly retreated. I simply needed (and need) someone with whom to share ideas. I need to explore and most fundamentally of all, perhaps, to test my ideas of a mother's love for her son and for my eternal yearning for such attention from a strong, motherly type: someone who would simply take me into her arms and let me lose myself. That comfort could be converted into bathing and later, other things perhaps. At this stage though, I now have this yearning for the maternal, which makes me look back at what has obviously been missed, and forward, to someone who might be able to fulfil that idea, at least in fantasy.

John.

March 14.
Dear John,

I decided to walk out of the meeting that I was in. I am too tired to focus. I am at my office now relaxing for an hour and will resume my work after I get a clear head. I thought if I were to write to you, it might help improve my outlook on things.

This morning and everyday really, as I leave the house, my son stands at the window and waves to me. I usually wave as I drive away. However, today I stopped the car, rolled my window and waved back. I took a long look at his little frame, his small hand and big, big smile as he was waving and felt my heart break into pieces. I was overwhelmed with feelings of pure sadness and fear of the future. I hurried and drove away in tears. I am so helpless. When August comes I have no idea how things will be. I feel very tired. Yes, I do feel very drained. I know that I am not losing my son. I know that I will see him periodically and he will be with me three months of the year. I will fight for this and will make sure that he knows me and bonds with me. He is so pure and so innocent. I want to see him always smiling and happy. He is lavished with love by his father. That comforts me in the sense that he will be well taken care of. So... I fall into despair and I come out of it like riding a roller coaster of fear and hope. Each plunge takes much of my energy.

Do you travel overseas much? Do you think you will ever come to NY? I was thinking if I were to meet you, how that would be? I thought it would be so strange. It seems to me like you are a voice in my head and to meet you would be such a strange materialisation of your physical reality. I am so happy to have you as a friend to talk to. Believe me... it means so much to me.

Simone.

March 14.

Dear Simone,

You are thanking me? It is I who should be thanking you! Look at my recent outpourings and the way you subtly encourage me. I can't believe we have come so far, so quickly! I have not travelled to the United States in many years. I dare not even think of such a thing. A meeting with you? It might be a disaster. It might be wondrous, but I dare not think of such potential dangers.

I do know though that you need to be held at this moment, held long and hard in a protective embrace. Whatever happens and whatever unfolds, please do not make any decisions when you are feeling at your lowest. This is not the way forward. Some people make decisions about emotional encounters when they are desperate. They then live to regret a lot. Wait until some of your strength is with you again, then make decisions. Try always to decide from a position of internal, emotional strength!

John.

7.

March 15.

John,

I know that every morning I rush with joy to see your response. It is so comforting to see that you have sent me something. Your last two e-mails have touched my heart. I do need to be held. I am so drained and so tired. I have not cried in a long time and every few days my emotions take a hold of me. I feel like bursting into tears but I hold myself (instead of *you* holding me; thank you for that sweet suggestion). I *do* have a lot of strength but also a lot of ability to bottle things away deep so they do not hurt me. I am not facing any of the reality of what is happening to me. I am slowly realising that my marriage has collapsed and I shudder at the mere thought. I do not know how I will survive when my son is taken from me. I am so tired. My husband is so cold to me these days. His only interest in me is sexual. He does not give me emotional support any more. I know that I have done things that caused us to drift but nothing that I have done was in a vacuum. I know myself and I know that what I was seeking was emotional comfort. I need to feel loved – to be held affectionately, with care.

Let me be frank. When he started to be less attentive to me, particularly on the emotional side, I drifted. I needed emotion. I found an alternative 'friend'. Betrayal works both ways but in the eyes of the law, I would certainly be presented as the guilty party! What could I do? Should I have betrayed my emotional integrity? He drifted as well. Yet, as I mentioned earlier, we continued to sleep together, to make love together – or more crudely, to fuck each other – because we both knew that, from that limited perspective, we were indeed 'a good fuck'! It sounds so sordid when presented like this but it is a fact.

Already, you mean so much to me. Your support is important and I am happy to know that my support means much to you. I do not feel lonely when I share my innermost thoughts and feelings with you. You need to share more with me about your emotions and feelings of emptiness. Why do you feel this way? Is it that you want to spare your wife the burden of your emotional needs? I long so much to be loved and feel that I will never be loved again. I know that is not the right thing to feel or say but I feel that the innocence of surrender to unconditional trust and having a man in my life who would be everything to me while I am everything to him is finished. It will never happen again. If I am to have any new relationship in my life, it would be spoiled with my realisation that it wasn't pure.

I need to go and get some sleep. I have one last question for you, and you may think it is strange but I will ask it anyway. If we were to meet, would we make love? Have you thought about this? I have. It would be pure, loving, and caring.

Simone

John was stunned to receive such a direct question. This was a woman he had befriended in cyberspace. This was a woman he had ambitions to imagine the strongest thoughts in his mind – to be cared for, bathed like a child and then to leap to manhood and be massaged to the point of ejaculation and ultimate forgiveness. On the face of it, this was not only a justification for his venturing into cyberspace, it was a potentially deep-seated vindication for his original motive. The fundament of his original motive was unshaken to this point. It was to be a world of ideas, hence the North American link, well away from a British reality.

March 17.

Simone,

I have denied myself any serious intimate thought of you in the sense of love-making. I deny the possibility in that I dare not even think of the vague yet tantalising notion of flying to NY. I wonder how the thought could even occur to me, and yet to say that the thought has not crossed my mind, fleetingly, would be a lie; plain and simple. I have not imagined the process of love-making with you, simply the idea of it. The process requires me to imagine what might actually happen. The idea is simply the principle; yes or no. I fight against such realism of 'process', fearing the deft articulation and beautiful consequences of such an occasion. I try and climb back into the clouds of the internet, inhabiting a nowhere world of ideas and dreams only.

My dilemma now is that you have prised open so much in me that you are in need of reward, even if that is only the dream world of erotic fantasy. Better to share such thoughts with another than to let it fester inside, turning mouldy and insidious with the contortions of conscience. Why, therefore, should I not yield to the beautiful temptation? I am simply trying to be careful – for my own peace of mind, for your equilibrium and our longer-term sustainability. It is clear that we offer one another so much!

You asked, "In your marriage, is it that you want to spare your wife the burden of your emotional needs?"

I once ventured vague ideas only to be dealt the blow of a grinding reality. I do not blame her. Having a disabled child is a crushing experience. No amount of love can avoid that reality. Only the strongest of people can cope with it. I may be determined but I do not feel particularly strong. Heather is strong but that attribute is totally consumed with the daily struggle to cope with the disappointments of losing her professional lifeblood, her sporting prowess and her hopes and fears for Andrew. I will honour that struggle in her and stay with her, for, in all other respects, we are the best of friends. In fact, you could say that we are like brother and sister: and that, my dear, is where additional problems start. Love-making is infrequent and when it is, it is very normal, even staid. I have so much more in me that needs to burst forth. I might be able to restrict that 'bursting' to the internet and you, but when you ask me about 'meeting' and therefore the inevitable possibility of lying together and behaving in ways ways we have only alluded to up to now, then perhaps you understand my caution. My other two children are fine. Life is not easy but it is not intolerable either. It just got on top of me at one point. For fear of repetition, I turned to friends and was thwarted and to my mind cruelly so, though unwittingly on their part. You appeared. To nurture this experience, we must be careful.

John.

March 20.

John,

Yes, we need to be careful with each other. I do not want to jump ahead and transform the beauty of our correspondence into something that will put it at risk. I have not had a chance to express myself freely in a while.

Even today, as I said, my mother and father are visiting and both my husband and I are keeping up a full facade as if we are happily married and nothing is wrong. The reason is that they are traditional Catholics and will not be able to deal with breakup. In my family, divorce is not an option, so I am not planning on letting them know my husband and I are separating. We may not end up divorcing anyway after all. We may lead the day-to-day existence but will not have what we once had in trusting each other and confiding to each other. I need time... lots and lots of time to fully understand what is happening to me.

I feel I am walking around like a zombie; I am alive but I

feel nothing. I do not feel loved. That is my basic problem. I am not loved and do not feel that I am appreciated. This feeling has had drastic, devastating results on me. Deep inside I know my husband does not love me any more but part of me is still resisting this realisation. Now, as my resistance is falling apart, I am going through hell!

Last night, I cried myself to sleep and this morning I woke up with tears. Now I am choking back tears as I am typing this e-mail. I know that I have to pull myself together and put on the show again when everyone wakes up.

I am tired of this.

Simone.

John read and re-read this passage. In divorce, he supposed, there would be hesitation, just like there was before a wedding. His impression was now that there has been 'sin', or at least fault, on both sides. What he still could not understand was why she was having to lose her son. This, after all, was the fundamental connection now between Simone and John. Her pain was to illustrate what might have happened to John's mother as she left him and vice-versa. His recalled pain was to help her understand her son's potential emotions on separating from his mother. The fact that other things had entered the picture seemed to satisfy an underlying need on both sides of this relationship. If these were contradictions upon contradictions, then so bit it. They simply conveyed the frailty of the human condition. They also heightened the obviously therapeutic nature of this extended conversation.

8.

March 24.

Simone,

Here is a little bit of early history to capture the frailty of emotional development.

'It had been a long time since he had touched the skin of a woman. It never occurred to him that this was abnormal or unusual. Whereas some parts of him were opening up, like his mind, the sexual and emotional side was closed. He was still too scared of things. Soon after college got into full swing, friends and groups began to form. Gloria was in one such group – a born teacher if ever there was one and a little older than some of the others. John became acquainted with her (and others), the result of which was an invitation to see her (and others) at her house. It turned out to be a mixed bag. First, the house was a Victorian two-storey upper floor apartment. Secondly, it was shared by another three women. One was a ballroom dancer whose boyfriend would appear at the house. So often it seemed as if he was a resident. Being the other half of the ballroom couple, they did everything in harmony. One wondered how they went to bed together. The sister was a stunner, with big breasts and a sensuous mouth.

This invitation seemed to coincide with a number of things. First, another of his fellow students was there – a man no less – and a relationship was blossoming between him and Gloria. Another was that one of the girls came with her boyfriend, also at the college. She was tall and athletic. She had long legs, the kind that could grip you in a vice of passion. The complication was that she was showing interest in John. Gloria told him. He was troubled by it. Having been at the wrong end of two marriage breakups, it simply wasn't in his makeup to become involved in another budding relationship. At this time, John was still in his puritan mode, no drinking, no swearing and indeed no women. Surely this could not last?

One of Gloria's ideas was for John to lose his virginity because he was almost twenty-one. The instrument for that loss was to be Cherie, the girl with the big breasts. He was invited to her room to talk, which was all John was expecting – his thinking still being on the simple side when it came to women. They started talking about nothing in particular, then John realized she was sitting casually on her bed. John did not move. After a bit, he left and rejoined the others. There were no tell-tale looks of inquiry.

The next time John visited the house, he was on his own. However, Cherie was not available because her boyfriend was around! John didn't understand the connection between them but clearly there was one.

Sometime later, John went there looking for Cherie. Was the time propitious? They went through the usual rituals and verbal gymnastics.

"If Bob finds out, he'll kill me," she said.

"Are you married?"

"No, but that's not the point!"

"What is the point?" he asked, being as patient as he could.

John began to wear her down, slightly. He was on the bed with her. They began to kiss. The groping phase came next. He started getting to the parts that mattered. There was the beginning of a sort of sexual contact. Then she stopped.

"I can't. I want to but I can't!"

John just looked at her and thought of things from her point of view. He stopped as well but still felt enlivened by the experience. He left and sped home on his motorbike, feeling elated though not relieved.'

John.

In the context of her emotional turmoil, he was trying to illicit a maternal response to his own faltered development – the cry to a mother figure. There was selfishness creeping into his side of the matter. His seemed to have a growing, if not already a constant, demand, for her attention, no matter what was happening to her. It was clearly a reflection of his own frailties. That could be an explanation but surely not an excuse. Anyway, this cyber-relationship with Simone was still in its early stages.

March 25.

John!

You write almost poetically about your own innocence. The sardonic touch of humour is masterful! I need to write to you about emotional love.

Emotional love is the most important thing to me. I noticed that over the past three years I lost interest in making love and considered it a chore rather than pleasure. Why? Because it has become mechanical, physical, non-spiritual; I do not feel loved. It is very important for me to feel loved emotionally. I do not have that blanket of comfort in my life any more. My husband thinks that I am too demanding in the expression of love. Yes, I do need a lot of emotional pampering, if you will. My expectations are very high. I am not talking about roses or gifts or any of that superficial stuff. I am talking about feelings and caring. Lack of emotional love breeds emptiness, isolation, lack of self-esteem and above all, depression. I guess both are important but which one is driving the other is what makes the difference.

The hardest times of the day to me are the early morning and when I go to bed. Sleeping through the night is a problem too. All I have now is my career.

I have started to worry as I know that come August, that's it. I am on my own. I have never been on my own. I have never handled bills or other financial issues. I worry that I will mess up my mortgage and not pay my bills on time or not have enough money for them at all. I never worried about my career and always carried myself with the air that if a job did not work for me, I would move on. I do not have that luxury now. I have started to worry about job security. I never did before!

I would like to hear from you about your feelings regarding intimacy. I would like to hear from you about the emotions that love-making either evokes or makes you long for in more detail. I have told you that emotional love is very important to me, but over the past three years all I experienced was just regular love-making. No rapture, no surrender, no elevation of my spirit or feeling of bonding and trust. It is not to say that it was not pleasurable, but it has not left any everlasting memories of fulfilment.

I am a very sensual woman and do enjoy making love passionately. I can tell you a little about my favourite things in making love. I love to be kissed and kissed and kissed so much. I like to be held and massaged all over my back, neck and shoulders. With oral, I do not like direct contact but a lot of soft kissing and licking around my neck and slowly down to my belly, lingering a bit two inches below my belly button. I like for the first contact to be very, very soft, as in little kisses barely touching me... then softly tasting me very, very softly, as if exploring. I like for the intensity to build up very gently. I do not like rapidity and harshness. I do enjoy oral sex a lot. However, I do enjoy conventional sex as well.

The feeling of male penetration is so perfect and fulfilling. It evokes emotions of protection and confidence. The initial moment of penetration, to me, is so delicious and precious. I like for a moment of pure stillness once a full penetration is achieved to take a deep breath and to feel the full depth and force of fulfilment. I like to be kissed during that time and to be able to breathe together.

Simone.

Whereas John was demanding attention through his sexual experiences, no matter how incomplete, he was now starting to wonder about his friendship with Simone. She bemoaned the absence of emotional love, often. She despaired at the mechanical side of lovemaking and yet... and yet, in the same breath, she was rejoicing in just that – the physical side of the process. It is therefore little wonder that John was inspired to respond to the physical side of things. This is what he seemed to excel at, certainly in his fictional writing.

9.

March 28.

John,

Would you please talk to me a bit more about your marriage? You must also tell me a little more about your emotional state in regards to sexual encounters. Some men are purely physical and have not much thought or emotions... not much to the idea of making love beyond the pleasure of the flesh. I am not saying that is bad but that is the state of emotion for such men. I think that you need to be loved so unconditionally and to be taken care of just like a child. You are a man and yet you need to be touched like a child. You have not yet found tenderness in being fully loved. I am not saying that I can provide you with this type of love. I think we are both in the same situation though. Please move more into your emotional consciousness and tell me more about who you are and what makes you happy.

If I were to meet you, I would not make love to you readily. I would cuddle you as a child, kiss you and hug as a child, hold your hands and softly sing you a lullaby as I pass my hand through your hair and hold you close to my heart. You do not have to please me sexually. I would more likely want to mother you and give you those lost emotions that you have never felt as a child. That is exactly what you need. I would channel my motherly energy into your being to protect you and quench the thirst of years that has been – and is still lingering – in your heart. Write me more... tell me about your dreams and hopes and desires.

Simone.

March 28.

Simone,

'I arrived at the hotel. I'd had a massage from her once before. A repeat performance suggested that she knew what she was doing and understood the needs of some.

"Hi! Oh hi! Now I remember you. Please excuse me. In this role, I meet so many and some even have a charming voice such as yours!"

She welcomed me to the room.

"Hard trip?"

"Very hard!" I replied.

"Well, you have the next couple of hours to relax and forget everything before you move on to other things."

The fold-away massage table was in position. Towels were arranged. I took my clothes off carefully, leaving them all on a chair. I was naked and saw my slightly tanned frame in the mirror. I felt good, if very tired indeed. I climbed on to the table, lying on my front, still naked.

"Would you like a towel?"

"Not really," I said. "Part of the pleasure of such an experience is to abandon all notions of control. The innocent nakedness is release in itself!"

"Good! I don't like having to mess about with additional bits bits of clothing and so-called carefully positioned towels anyway. It interferes with what I feel should be done."

Her hands worked first on my back. She worked and worked and worked, eventually moving up to my shoulders.

"Ah, there's a lot of tightness in here, far too much tension!"

She massaged and pressed and found those magic spots that somehow released whatever stress was inside. My mind drifted, as it should in such a context of total abandonment. I became aware of things as she moved to my calves and rear thighs, then my feet – uncharacteristically ticklish. She finally moved to my buttocks, massaging, massaging, massaging. She reached to my inner thigh. I flinched slightly with the potential of it all.

"Are you all right?"

"I'm more than all right; this is lovely!"

Her hands were skillful. She knew that I was beginning to respond.

"What's on your mind?"

I hesitated, then told her, because I felt I could trust her.

"What's on my mind?" I said as her fingers continued to work my inner thighs. "I think of your hands moving directly to my ass, to its gentle caress and other things..."

As soon as the words tripped out, she was using her nails, very gently, to induce additional sensation.

"Oh, my heavens!" I whispered.

"Are you all right?"

"Mmmmmmmmm."

"What else do you feel?"

"That you could do anything to me, that you could use a finger and penetrate."

I suddenly realised what I had been induced to say, through total relaxation and an increasing focus on my ass-rim. "I'm sorry! Was that wrong?"

"Shush! Just relax!" and as I did, she lubricated a little more and started pushing a finger in. She could tell I was loving it.

"Please, I would only ever ask for such a thing if I knew you enjoyed it. I would hate to feel this happening from a person who didn't like it."

"Don't worry. I like it. I wouldn't do it if I didn't."

With that, I closed my eyes as she pushed her finger in deeper and deeper, with the fingers of her other hand caressing the outer edges of my balls. I pushed my ass up a little to allow for increased access all round. It felt wonderful.

"Turn over please." I woke to the request, turned to reveal my partial erection. She oiled her hand some more, then encouraged my manhood to full stature.

"Can I watch you?" I asked. "It adds to the thrill of it."

"Yes!"

I did, and as I propped myself on my elbows to get slightly closer, I felt again her finger in deep penetration and her hand working my cock to its splendour. Even for me, it looked majestic.

"Pull one knee up."

I understood the purpose and obeyed. "Do you want to use use two fingers?"

She nodded and smiled, left my cock and started pulling my ass apart to ensure a smooth and larger penetration. She pushed and pushed again until she was firmly and deeply inside. With her other hand, she took my cock again and started to work it harder and harder.

I touched her bare arm; her skin was so smooth.

"Do you mind?" She smiled again, confirming that things were okay. I suddenly found myself under her loose-hanging blouse, caressing a bra-less breast and nipple.

"I'm sorry, I'm sorry!"

She smiled again, telling me, "It's all right, really." As her cock-consuming hand started working its magic, I started blurting expletives, then realised what I was saying.

"Sorry, sorry! It just adds to the excitement of it all! Do you mind?"

Again she smiled. "No, I don't mind." As those words were converted into rougher phrases, I began to come.

"Oh God, oh God!"

As my excitement peaked with my climax, she said,

"You've got a beautiful dick!"

Its beauty was suddenly confirmed as I exploded.

"Oh my God, you fucking gorgeous woman!"

I moved into an immediate post-ejaculation flush. She smiled and told me to lie flat and relax.

"Let me get a warm towel." She brought it and embraced

my manhood, cleaning the head and the residue surrounding it.

She then resumed with the rest of my front massage – front thighs, feet, head, and chest. As I relaxed in the totality of abandonment, we had come to the end of my scheduled time.'

John.

March 30.
John,

Your e-mail has left me breathless…. You are so lovely! What delicacy and what revealing aspects of penetration. I never knew massages could be so full of satisfaction. You are full of surprises! Lovely surprises! Please stay in my life.

Simone.

John's apparent selfishness appeared to pay off. It certainly seemed to endear him to Simone. She loved the description. It left her 'breathless'. More to the point perhaps, it distracted her from her own travails. Furthermore, if she liked writing about penetration and oral sex, then he assumed that she enjoyed reading about it. At this point, though, whether real or fictitious, it did not matter. It was an interesting development.

March 30.
Dear John,

What a wonderful day you have given me. You are so special and so beautiful in your own unique way. I have a couple of traits that I have been blessed with and I have only recently become conscious of them.

First, I have come to rediscover my being a sexually and and physically attractive woman. I never thought of myself in such terms and never carried myself in such a manner either. When I was young, I was a very focused and serious student. I always felt more comfortable with my mental ability versus my being attractive. I have realised this very recently and you may laugh at this but it is really true. My mother was very harsh in raising us – always stressing manners, education, and being serious. I have come to notice that I do turn heads when among people. I do not walk or talk or do anything to raise such energy but it happens often at work. I never noticed this until recently. I suppose this realisation stems from my pending divorce and its legality of freedom. I have started looking at other men, realising that all harbour some positive potential. It is a form of liberation, I suppose.

Secondly, my other trait is that I have an unbelievable level of optimism and strength of will. I feel that there is nothing that I cannot achieve if I want to and I put my mind to it. When I came to the US, I was in awe with the advances here. I found this country to be so wonderful. The level of openness and freedom was so incredible. If I were to love you, I would shower you with much affection and care. I have been really, really hurt in knowing that I have become the object of my husband's desire but that our love just disappeared over the years. I have asked myself why this happened. The reason, I was told, is practicality, marriage, blame game and so on. I do not feel special any more and at many times I felt that we are in the marriage only because it was convenient. That realisation was like acid that kept on smouldering in my spirit.

I could not make love for a year after my son was born. It was physically painful and I truly hated it. At the end of that year, I asked for a divorce and my husband agreed. We separated for four months, and, as we were planning the financial aspects, we decided to not go through with it for many reasons, but love was not one of them. I need to be loved! It is so painful to not feel loved. The sharing of a soft laugh, a whisper, a touch... holding each other gently and just drawing breaths together is so, so wonderful. I have tremendous ability to love and to express that love in many ways, not only physically.

I do feel a very strong motherly love for you. I am emotionally unfocused now, and I need you to help me. I need you to hold me and to tell me that it will be all right. I need your support and to confide in me about your personal erotic discoveries. I want us to have a very special place in our hearts for each other. Already, I have a place in my heart for you. If that can be considered motherly love in a special way, then you are truly loved. I want to mother you. I want you to feel my unconditional care and support with or without sexual pleasure. I want you to come to me so I will hold you near to my heart. If you feel like crying, it is fine. I will kiss your tears. I will rub your back, shoulders, arms and cuddle you very warmly and tell you that you are the best and t h a t you are safe between my arms. When you are hurt, you will ask me to make it feel better, just like my baby does, and

I will kiss you and hope it will make you feel better.

We have come a long, long way this past week. Are you you emotionally tired? I feel such strength because you are in my life. I will share much more with you and I have big hopes for us. I believe in you, so please believe in me. Stay with me and I will stay with you. I will heal you and rejuvenate your tired spirit. I know that loving you is part of healing you. I have my arms very wide open for you, so come to me and I will hold you very, very close to my heart. You will feel my warmth and loving energy. Be safe and happy. I will cover you with a warm blanket of soft kisses and give you the fullness of my breasts to suckle your weakness into strength. Do not be afraid or lonely... I am here.

Simone.

April 2.

Dear Simone,

'You beckoned me into the bedroom. I needed to be wanted. I needed to be comforted. You knew it. Your en-suite bathroom looked warm. Its lights were pink, very feminine, and why not? It was yours.

"Come here, John. Let me help you."

As I walked through the door, I could hear the water rushing and see the steam rising. It was very cold outside; it was a typical December day in New York. The window was steaming up. I wanted to keep that feeling of total enclosure. You unbuttoned my shirt and pulled it from my trousers. You saw my chest and looked surprised. My pectorals were subtle yet well formed. I had the physique of a swimmer though I had never been a swimmer. You pulled up a chair and sat in front of me. You opened my belt and let my trousers fall to the floor. The doorbell rang.

"Sorry, John! Just get into the bath. I wonder who that can be?"

I took off the rest of my things, dipped my toes in and realised that the water was too hot. I poured in more cold. The bath salts gave a wonderful scent. I lowered myself into the water.

"Who was it?" I asked as you returned.

"You wouldn't believe it. It was a pizza man with a delivery. He was lost; the address was wrong. I felt so sorry for him that I took it and paid him. We can have pizza after!"

With that, you moved to your knees on a towel.

"How do you feel?" you asked.

I was half asleep and murmured relaxed pleasure. You took the soap and started caressing my shoulders. I loved it. You rubbed some more. It was bliss.

"Stand up please and let me wash your back properly."

An erection was already forming. You stood and took your soapy hands to my shoulder blades and lower back. You rubbed gently before sliding both hands round my waist. My skin tingled with excitement.

You moved down to my legs and wrapped each thigh in turn, in care and soap. I was melting with your touch. I didn't know what would happen next...'

Would you simply ask me to sit down and rinse off? Would you ask me to turn a round, thus revealing to you, by now, my pulsating manhood? Would the sight of it shock or excite you? Would you embrace and consume it in many ways? I wonder.

At a moment like this, abandon is truly exciting.

John.

John's profile was becoming clear. His level of emotion was limited to the assurance from Simone that he would not be admonished for his physical desires. He expressed no love himself, just the want of love through his very narrow focus: the physical, the mechanical, even the vaguely exhibitionist – simply wanting to be seen.

April 3.

Dear John,

You give me such comfort and now even delightful surprises that make me smile. Yes, you are naughty, you know. I do not know what to tell you or which option I would choose in real life. I love the idea of bathing you though! I love the idea of towelling you as well. I would love to cover you with a warm towel and to rub your head, and as I remove the excess water from your hair and face and when I bring it down your shoulders, I would see your glistening clean face dashing with a bright smile. I will know that I have given you much happiness and I will smile back and shower your face with lots and lots of kisses. As I towel you further and further – yes! I would notice your erection. I would give you a warm smile and gently towel you there further, slower and gentler. I would take you with my hands and gently caress you, feeling your hardness and holding you close until it dissipates.

As I told you, I would not make love to you yet. I want to mother you first. I want to give you much motherly love. In time, I do not know. Maybe I would make love to you. I am not sure, but, right now, I see you as a child. You are my precious loving child waiting for me to hold and to take care of you.

Let me tell you a little about yesterday. I went to the gym, for my first workout. I took a yoga class and will continue to do so from now on. I have just finished a Tai Chi class and learned the first nineteen forms and three stances. It is a good exercise to release my energy and calm my spirit.

Today, I went there again after a day of intensive cleaning that left me so tired. I spent an hour on a stationary bike. I have to go now.

Write me John. I love your e-mails.

I held you close to me last night and softly sang you a song so you would sleep.

Simone.

10.

April 6.

Dear Simone,

You make me melt. You make me feel soft inside and in need to be wrapped in your arms. I need to feel that totality of unencumbered love that only a mother can provide. In such arms my various torments would disappear. I would feel the curve of your breasts and want to drink from them. I would certainly want to feel the warmth of the flesh that embraces such inner beauty. I would want to climb into you, from whence I came, and start all over again.

Out I come. 'It's a boy!' they would exclaim and, after being cut and washed, I would be placed upon your breast. My suckling would start and I would remain there forever. I trust none but you; no other living, breathing creature comes close to you. It is just you. My world is nothing but you. I live, breath, eat, and sleep simply for you.

I am astonished at such free-form writing! Do I disturb you? There is obviously something deep-seated that needs to come out.

John.

April 6.

Dear John,

We have been corresponding for a bit over twenty days! I am overwhelmed. I do not have feelings of love in the classical sense for you. I do have motherly, loving feelings and I do hope that does not depress you or make you close your loving feelings to me. I do want to take care of you "virtually" and listen to everything that you have to say to me. This correspondence is so precious to me and I do not want to jeopardise it. Do you see the difference? Why do you feel so much love for me?

I can see in you the child I am losing today and for that I love you in a very motherly way and want to give you what you need to heal you and to protect you. I do not want to make love to you since I know that will confuse you. You have most of your life been reaching out to women physically. I want you to reach out to me emotionally. You do not have to please me sexually and you do not have to desire me. I do want to hold you as a mother and to bathe you as a mother, to comb your hair and to dress you as a mother, to sing to you a song as a mother, to give you that which you lost years and years ago.

Your love for me is strong and very passionate. I understand that and I know that you are trying to analyse it. It is not physical but that is the only way that you have learned to express your desire for protection and security. I will give you that without having to go through the physical act of love-making. I want to give you comfort and shelter you.

Think... think about the powers of the universe and what opportunity they have given you and me. It is not a coincidence. It is not a stroke of luck or the hands of random chance. I am in your life to heal you and that is what I want to do. Healing you is loving you but not 'making love' to you. It is so ephemeral to make love... I am so tempted to accept your physical love. It is so sensual and so delicious how you write and what you describe.

If I were to extend my virtual reality to you, then I would cuddle you and caress you. I would caress all of you. I would give you all the love that you would have been given had you not lost your mother. Please do not take my response as rejection. I am opening a different door for you in my life. Other women have given you one door; that of desire. I want to give you a totally different level of loving that is so pure and unconditional. It is the strangest thing but I do feel as if you are truly my child. Can you imagine that? I am astounded at my feelings. I could just close my eyes and feel your spirit hanging around me... a naughty four year old playing with his toys and asking so many questions.

My son screams when I force him to take a bath! He just hates it. I hug him and kiss him and rub his face and body and just shower him with loving kisses as he tells me his magical stories of monsters and how he "hit all the monsters". I grieve as I know that I am soon to lose these innocent moments.

I will kiss you and kiss you and shower you with hugs and kisses as a loving mother.

Be patient, John. You are so bright and so unique. I do not

know what is happening to me and I do not understand our communication either, but I am happier than I was before. Please be here for me.

Simone.

April 17.

Dearest John,

I went to sleep early last evening and woke up tossing and turning. I spent the night holding my son in my lap and smelled his hair and kissed his forehead as he wiggled and asked me to not kiss him as he is now a big boy! I laughed and cried as I heard his soft voice in protest. I looked deeply in his eyes and could only wonder what will come next. What is awaiting him in life? What will he do when he wakes up in the night and I am not there? Will there be another strange woman that will take my place and what will she do when he cries? Oh, John, my heart is just breaking with sadness. I wish I could continue this marriage but I cannot. I wish I could keep him but I know that I cannot. I rejoice in knowing that I will have him three months of the year but that is so little and I will miss so many critical points in his life. Will he end up hating me? Will he end up feeling that I let him down? I am so confused.

I have very dark thoughts that are consuming me. I feel like I am drowning in deep, dark, cold icy water. I reach out with my hands up but there is nothing but death and darkness. I need you to hold me so I can cry and cry and cry for years of pain.

Tonight, I imagined that I let you slip into my bed. I held you and you felt the warmth of my bed sheets. You curled curled up and held on to me feeling the sweetness of safety between my arms.

It was not sexual. We felt nothing but peace and security. You were a little angel with bright eyes peering into mine. You had little arms and very small feet almost touching my knees. You clung to me in the dark of night, fearing nothing and relishing the warmth of my body. I heard you breathe softly. I kissed your forehead as I pulled you closer.

There are so many complex things that are happening to me. I need to be strong. Whenever I feel weak I will come to you. It is such a paradox. You are my escape and my relief.

Let me tell you a little more about my recent history. Of course, as you know, my husband and I finally agreed to divorce in February. We knew that our marriage was at an end. These things are funny though, because one cannot say for sure when and how a marriage dies. It is like a snake that lies still then suddenly jumps to bite you. You knew that it was there all along but you just could not scream in surprise when the attack came. I had an affair with a married man three months ago, seeking emotional love. I sought validation and affirmation that I am special, and that I would still have a chance to be loved. I broke off the relationship on Friday. I did not want him to break up his marriage although he is very unhappy, just as I am. All I wanted was for us to love each other very passionately. I only saw him five times. The last time was very special. It was so sweet. I experienced such pleasure and such joy in his arms. However, I began to have doubts about his emotional attachment to me, which is why I had to end it. On Friday I sent him an e-mail and told him that I did not wish to continue our affair. I have not heard from him since.

The reason I decided to break it off is that he does not really understand me. When we talked of love, he was worried that I wanted him to leave his family! I told him that I did not want that to happen and would never have asked him to do so. All I wanted was for him to love me and spend more time with me! I was confused. Did he really love me or simply find me extremely erotic? He said that I have too many expectations from a man.

Why am I telling you these things? These are most complex of times in my life. I need you to hold me and tell me that it is all right. I want to be loved, John. Is that so much to ask for? I am not talking about mere physical interaction but strong emotional rapture and undying all-consuming love. I want to be one with my beloved. I need to be one in spirit and one in body. I want him to be my shelter and I his. For years, I have accepted my empty life, and I am so tired now. I feel like a very empty shell that has become broken and neglected. I need to be filled with happiness and life. I wish you were here. I could curl up between your arms and go to sleep as you tell me that tomorrow is a better day.

Simone.

11.

John was delving further and further into Simone's mind. She had evoked not only sympathy but also passion from him. Her expressions of passion were laced with the feminine imperative of emotion. For one reason or another, his thoughts were focused less on the emotions of the exchanges, save those of the need for a mother figure. Instead, his was a hunger for physical description to flow from his mind and, ideally, to read the same from her. His wish was granted.

April 10.

Dear John,

'You are sound asleep. I enter your room very quietly and walk to your bed. I turn on the light and set it to dim. You are still sleeping. I sit at the side of your bed and hear you breathe. I admire your peaceful trance and brush my hands against your hair. I lean and kiss your forehead gently and hold your hand.

You open your eyes slowly and see me there, so you give

me a big smile. I smile back at you. You pull yourself up and I come closer and hold you. You bury your nose in my hair and the smell of my perfume covers you. I give your neck several little kisses and move up to your ear. I whisper softly in your ear, "I miss you! Do you miss me?" You answer me with a kiss on my shoulder as you hold me closer, much, much closer. My breath is softly brushing against your cheeks. You part your lips to meet mine. Our lips are barely touching yet softly they meet each other. We breathe together. Our tongues touch. I love your taste. Our lips are tightly embracing each other. Long, passionate, soft wet kisses leave us both breathless.

I am wearing a long lacy night gown. You can see the beauty of my body through the soft layers. It has two buttons on the front. Your hands have already found them. You slowly unbutton my gown and slip it down off of my shoulders. Your hands brush against my arms. You hold me back and take a deep look at my breasts, full of warmth and desire for you. You reach and caress me and pull me to your bare chest. Our hearts are beating together. I feel so safe and protected in your arms.

I tell you, "You are so special to me, my precious darling John; hold me tight." You do hold me tight. My head is on your shoulders and my arms are wrapped around your neck. You are so warm. I kiss you on your forehead, eyes, lips, chin; you totally surrender to my soft lips. You know that you are loved and safe. I kiss your shoulders and lay you on the bed. I slowly kiss you from your chest down to your belly button. As I go down, you can feel my breasts brushing against your body. You love the silky feeling and it stirs your desire for me.

I linger two inches below your belly button, licking you in little circles. My tongue sends waves of pleasure across your body. You are overtaken with passion for me. I can feel your hardness now. I cup your manhood with my hands and kiss you. I can feel your desire. I look at you and smile very warmly as I admire your manhood so hard and erect, just for me.

I kiss your head softly. I taste a drop of your pre-cum – so delicious and fragrant. I massage your shaft and balls. You are full of passion and ache for my lips to taste you. I lick your head very gently and go down your shaft to your balls. You feel waves of thunder down your spine and moan with desire. I spread your legs wide and take you into my mouth. You feel the warmth of my touch and raise your hips in anticipation and ecstasy. I push you down as I suck and lick you vigorously. One hand is holding your shaft as I taste your beauty and the other caresses your balls. You are in rapture, totally surrendering your heart, mind, body and spirit to me. I have you between my hands wrapped with loving desire so delicately and so preciously. You are mine.

I do not want you to cum yet so I slow down and pull towards you. I am on top of you and take your manhood and guide it inside me; hmmmmmm. It feels so wonderful to have you inside me. I close my eyes and take a deep breath as I feel your fullness penetrated so deeply. Your heart is throbbing. I want to ride you so badly, but I wait.

We breath and slow down. You feel my womanhood so warm

and juicy. I pull a little, just a little to adjust myself; I fall back. You feel the strength of my desire. I hold your hands and lean a little as your lips meet my nipples. I push my head back moaning with deep, long desire. Your lips feel great and I start to move slowly up and down your shaft. As you speed your sucking, I speed my rhythm. I ride you hard, up and down, as we both expend our energy and suddenly feel the tide of passion exploding. We cum together.

I fall on your chest, breathing very fast as I feel your manhood throbbing inside me. I hold you as you raise your hips for a deeper insertion. I writhe with pleasure. I am so happy. You are so happy too. I pull all the way as you gasp softly – more pleasure. I lie next to you. You cover me and we sleep tightly next to each other.'

Simone.

With this level of writing, John felt that this whole cyber-exploration was now, not only vindicated, but also a triumph of mutual exploration! How could he not? To read such descriptions was deeply satisfying. This may have been a sad reflection of John as an emotional being but his feelings were simple evidence of a series of insights and experiences that he would not have had otherwise. Perhaps if he had been in therapy, with a mature woman, of course(!), maybe all this would have tumbled from his mouth and on to her notebook. There was no therapy – not of the official kind anyway. If the truth be known, this cyber-relationship was his therapy. It was uncovering things within himself that he simply did not know existed. He had never written like this before and certainly not in an erotic manner. Simone had already acknowledged a few times that, according to her, his erotic writing was skilful. At this stage, the erotic was laced with a maternal undertone – the need to be loved, no matter what his transgression might be. In this case, the transgression was that of expressing the need to touch and be touched, to see and be seen – whether in the bathroom (the original – indeed, innocent – ambition) or the bedroom (moving to another level).

She gave him more!

12.

April 14.

John,

'Tonight, I want to give you a bath. You are sitting at your desk working away. I walk to you and stand behind your back. I hold your hands and lean my head forward to your ear and whisper, "Darling, it is time for your bath." You look at me and smile. The room is warm, and I have already set up everything. I have poured hot water into the tub. I have lit a few candles and folded your towel on the chair. The mirrors are fogged up as the steam fills the room. I hold your hand and you turn around.

You are wearing a pair of pants and a shirt. I take your arm and unbutton one sleeve; I caress your palm. I reach with my other hand and brush your face. Your eyes speak to me of long years of restlessness and pain. I lean forward and kiss you between your eyes and tell you, "It is okay... I am here." I wrap my arms around your head and you bury it in the folds of my chest and you hug me. I tell you, "It is okay my precious child... let go. I am here." I feel the saltiness of your tears streaming silently as I comb your hair with my hands and gently kiss your head. I whisper softly,

"Hush. Don't cry. I am here."

I keep on softly kissing you and my lips feel the saltiness of of your tears. I hold your chin and pull your head up. You look into my eyes. I am smiling at you. You ask me, "Do you love me?" I tell you, "You are so precious, my sweet angel. Yes, I do."

You smile. I unbutton your shirt and pull it down slowly. You sit quietly watching me. I fully undress you. You stand up and I hold you. The aroma of the candles fills the room with the scent of lavender. It is time, my angel.

I walk you to the tub and help you in. You feel the warmth of the water as it relaxes your tired muscles. I kneel in front of you and caress you. I slowly bathe your shoulders, arms, chest, and back. You close your eyes. I reach between your legs. You tense a bit. I tell you to relax. You do. I spread your legs and slowly wash you there. You tell me how lovely it feels.

You are so clean and so fresh. It is time to sleep now. I walk you to your bed, tuck you in. You are very tired. I hold your hand and dim the light. I softly sing you a song. I kiss you gently on your forehead as you fall asleep. I linger there for a few moments, admiring you, then I turn off the light and walk away.'

Simone.

John felt as though he was in heaven. This was the second recent outpouring of erotic thoughts – in truth, converted into a maternal sensuality – towards him. It was as though he had arrived! His ambition for something in Yahoo Personals –

reading those 'cries for help' – and recognizing his own, had now blossomed into something almost stunning. It was certainly a revelation. More importantly perhaps, it built an anticipation and excitement in his life that was not a feature of his recent existence in marriage. The marriage itself was mundane, yet pleasant enough. It was a complacent form of living; something he assumed to be the norm for mere mortals. There was no passion. When John reflected on his cyber-behaviour and therefore, the conventional notion of betrayal, he rationalized the whole thing by wondering if what he experienced with Simone might magically transfer itself back to his now sexually dormant relationship with Heather. He had nothing but care for her. Yet care is not the same as passion.

April 16.

John,

You are aware and conscious of your desires emotional and sexual. In the context of your reality you cannot achieve such liberation. You are locked in a functional marriage that is basically devoid of spirit. I was too. I lived, ate, slept, cooked and worked mechanically. I was so unhappy because I knew there is no love in my life.

Now, I feel good that I am free. I can express my discontent about the vacuum in my heart. You are exploring that vacuum too. Do not be alarmed! I am not saying that you should end your marriage. Please do not misunderstand me. I am saying that you are discovering the too frequent bondage of marriage. Some people just accept it and continue living, sometimes with sporadic affairs to compensate for the feeling of emptiness.

Other people choose to end the marriage, and some just accept what life has given them. However, as we have been corresponding more, I feel that there is more that you are looking for. You might be able to articulate it or not. It could be an inner feeling or primitive survival need or insecurity. I do not know but it is different. Please open up to me, John. I want to embrace you and be open to your dreams, thoughts, and possibly just by being that for you, I might help you find your inner peace.

Make love to me passionately and gently. Consume me in your thoughts and express your desire to melt with me. Be who you want to be; I am here for you. I am here to receive you. I feel we have only just started. No restraint please. This is so exciting!

Simone.

What was he to think now? He was ecstatic. He read and re-read the message. He was in cyber-heaven.

13.

April 21.

John,

Have you ever dreamt about having more than one woman in bed with you at the same time? Does this thought raise your erotic intensity? Have you ever experienced such a thing? What do you think of it? Or have you ever thought of sharing one woman with another man? I have never experienced such a thing. I wonder if it gives one more intense pleasure than a twosome would. I get a very erotic sensation when I think of such things. I know that it is very naughty but I do! I am blushing now. I am actually feeling a surge of sensation between my legs when I think of such things. It must be sensational and exhilarating to experience such a thing. What do you think? I must go now. Please write me. It lifts my spirits when I hear from you.

Bye.

For John, this message was another watershed. He was stunned. Had he uncovered something in her that was always there? Had he prompted her to think of such things for the first time? Either way, the maternal belief was now giving way to a different kind of woman. This was now a woman who wanted to push the frontiers of thought, maybe even into action. The fact that she was willing to consider herself with another woman and man (the classic threesome, from the male standpoint), was selfishly acceptable to him – why on earth would it not be? Yet, having herself 'taken' by two men struck a sinister chord in his mind. This may be (selfishly) acceptable to her (and why on earth should it not be if all enjoyed the experience?) but it struck a sinister chord in him. The word 'jealously' appeared for the first time in his lexicon. He assumed that she would be one of the two women, not that she would simply watch two other women with a man. Maybe she had lesbian tendencies or at least that she could 'swing both ways'. He wasn't making any judgment in that regard.

Then she ventured the idea of John sharing a woman with another man. Again, he assumed that this was her desire, if only a latent one. It smacked of her wanting to be dominated by two men. What other connotation could there be? In such a situation, the woman would be overpowered and be overwhelmed with the two men's physical strength and subsequent ejaculations, whether into her or simply on to her. Either way, his breath left him for a moment out of shock. His underlying thought boiled down to the idea that domination could actually be a desire for something worse, to be taken against her will. If not, then certainly to be overpowered in the course of being taken, knowing of course, that her single or even multiple orgasms would be assured! It was dangerous territory and he felt uneasy with this move into experimentation, in which – he supposed – he was not the sole partner!

April 25.

My dear Simone,

I think I am pushing the boundaries of our imaginings, the limits of what is possible. Then you come up with such an electrifying question! Being in bed with a woman and another man sends shudders of jealousy through me. The very thought of it repels in all respects. Then comes the hypocrisy of it all – man and two women? That is something entirely plausible, comfortable, selfish and acceptable. I know this, because I have had this experience. This is not too shocking, I hope.

John.

April 25.

Dear John,

I agree with you. I would not really be interested in sharing myself with two men. I believe that there would be too much masculine energy and that I would not feel comfortable. In all honesty, the scenario that presents itself to my imagination is a threesome with two women and a man. I think that would be much more pleasurable. As I said, I have never experienced this. I think about it and, each time, it gives me a tingling sensation. I sensed that you did have such experiences! I felt it. I would love to hear about them and your impression of the whole experience. My, my, John, we really have come very far in our communication. I am astounded that I can open up like this and share these most intimate thoughts with you. I am smiling now. I know that I am in good hands though and for that you get a kiss and a big hug.

Simone.

April 27.

Simone,

'I was sitting on a hotel terrace in nowhere land. Two gorgeous women came and sat near to me but not at my table. I pretended to read but looked over at them with increasing interest. They responded, and soon we were sitting together. We started talking. One girl was on the verge of moving to Denmark to join her new husband. The other was a local hairdresser. The first girl (let's call her Leyla) was tall and upright. Her breasts were full; her smile, warm. The other (Beatrice – I remember her because I saw her a few more times on her own) was smaller and slightly fatter but with a beautiful cleavage and a sensual smile. We got to know each other a little and then decided to go up to my room.

We entered and they got their bearings. They took their shoes off and sat on the bed. They beckoned me to sit with them.

"How on earth do I please both of you?" I asked naively.

"Just relax," they said.

I turned one way and kissed Leyla. She tasted like a gorgeous woman should. I turned and kissed Beatrice – another perfect kiss. With that first physical connection established, they started taking their clothes off. As they were doing so, they started pulling at me. I was already full of desire, with a rock hard erection. I moved to Leyla and helped her with her bra. Her black and beautiful breasts were so rich and (almost) so full of milk. I started sucking with care. Yet I still aware of Beatrice and with my free hand searched for her and found myself already stroking her.

Kissing and sucking a beautiful breast was one thing but caressing the pussy of another woman seemed to be absolutely electrifying, and we hadn't even really started yet. It was clear that they had done this before and that Leyla was the dominant of the two. I decided to concentrate on her and hoped Beatrice would follow. I even told her to, in gentle terms. I wanted to kiss Leyla all over and so I did. Her face, her breasts again, her belly and then – how delicious – her pussy; all were consumed. She opened it all wide with her fingers and shoved my face into it. I stayed there kissing and sucking. I still had a free hand and was searching for Beatrice. She had moved round and taken my shaft, and after massaging it for a few moments, she moved round to my buttocks. I was still drowning in the juice and moans of pleasure from Leyla. Beatrice started to lick my balls from behind, caressing and wetting the crease between my ass. She then took my shaft and slipped it into Leyla's mouth.

I tried to resist coming at once and even managed it for a little. Beatrice was still licking and caressing my balls. I was still, sucking and drinking and pushing my tongue into Leyla as far as it could go. I felt I was not on this planet.

"Fuck me now!" Leyla insisted suddenly.

I was pulled out and again Beatrice performed the

service of putting me into Leyla's pussy. Even at that time, I would try and hold things up. Then it started; the hard, hard repetitive penetration. I was on top but kept my body up high with the strength of my arms. I manoeuvred so that I could watch my shaft slipping in and out of her.

"Look!" I said.

"Is that not beautiful? Watch it slide in and out."

Both did briefly and just laughed with pleasure. Then it was time; I could hold on no longer.

Serious, rhythmic fucking started. Added to this was Beatrice kissing Leyla and holding my back, helping me to push! She loved watching! On and on I went, and finally the beauty of the experience came pouring out. I was pulled out suddenly and pushed back into her mouth. She wanted everything!

I was giggling with boyish exhilaration. The first round was so beautifully done. (I have the ability, sometimes, to recover fairly quickly. When that happens, the second time is much longer and more sustained. Such was the situation this time.)

We were lying together, me in the middle. I moved to the point where each hand was able to find their pussies. For a few minutes, I was able to treat them equally. But Beatrice was now getting a little restless. By coincidence, my blood was pumping again and within (what seemed) no time at all, I was ready and almost being pushed on to the lovely smooth skin and very full breasts of Beatrice. I tried to kiss and suck her pussy but she was now impatient. Leyla positioned me, kissed my shaft, licked it to make it wet, and then pushed me into

Beatrice. I started as she wanted and pumped away for what seemed like ages. It just felt like (excuse the phrase) a fucking performance of such pure efficiency. Beatrice began to writhe with pleasure. Leyla moved up and opened her mouth. Beatrice arched her head back. They dripped fluid and teased each other's tongues. I did not come – that was not the point. What mattered was that Beatrice did. I was so pleased for her and proud of myself. Now, I was tired.

I lay down and after a moment Leyla positioned herself with her head on my inner leg, within sucking range.

"I just love to suck you!" she said and started.

I lay there, with Leyla sucking my still firm shaft. I was lying flat so Beatrice came round and placed her pussy over my mouth. My tongue came out of my mouth. I licked and sucked her as I was being licked and sucked. I tasted a mixture of her fluid and mine. If heaven were a position, it would be that one, with me and two women both being satisfied with unadulterated pleasure – one positioned at one end of my body and one at the other. I began to feel the slow deep movement of some fluid starting to move through my balls and into my shaft.

"I'm going to come!" I called out, through Beatrice's open legs.

Leyla moved again so that she would catch it in her mouth and over her chin. This was a slow one; I savoured it. The excitement grew and grew and grew until it was time to flow out gently: no wild spurting this time, just the even surges of a wonderful orgasm. Leyla caught and sucked the fluid as it flowed slowly out of the tip of my head. Now it was over. We just lay there, lingering in the darkness of the evening. I asked if Leyla was all right. She moved lazily and kissed my chest.

"Are you okay, Beatrice?" She rolled even closer and kissed my shoulder. We were done, so beautifully and completely done.'

John.

14.

May 1.

John,

I do not think that I would enjoy something like this. I felt very empty after I read your description. I am not sure why but it filled me with sadness and loneliness to read your words. Maybe it is because I am tired. I think, on some level, I felt these ladies did not really lend themselves to you emotionally but only physically. I would never be able to do such a thing. I think that I would be cold if I did not share my emotions with you. Are you sad, John? I feel that you are feeling empty too. Did you feel tired and drained after you wrote that e-mail to me? I feel somewhat unsettled now that I have read your description. Maybe I was not ready for such a description of a raw level of physical exchange. It seemed to me so mechanical and so lacking of spiritual concern.

John, we have come a long way, don't you think?

My early days before I married my husband were magical. He taught me the pleasures of sex. As I said before, he was the first to experience oral sex with me. Of course, I never thought or imagined that men also would enjoy a similar thing. I would not have even imagined that such things happened. He gently introduced me to oral pleasure and was very loving with me. Over time I felt that he wanted me to pleasure him in the same way as well. I hesitated and just could not imagine myself getting over such a shock barrier. However, I loved him so much and wanted to give him pleasure. One time after he had pleasured me, I just dropped down to my knees and started kissing his belly. I could see that he was so electrified with anticipation. I held his shaft and slowly licked and sucked the head. His back arched with desire. It felt great to give him such pleasure. I cupped his balls. I could feel the surge of his climax. I loved his taste and I felt so much closer to him – more than ever in my life. We hugged each other and he kissed me so passionately in his appreciation.

You see, John, all my life, loving and sex were two identical sides of the same passion. I feel that I am starting to love you and in that I am opening up to you physically. It is very strange for me to love you. I have never met you but I feel such a bond with you that I cannot explain. There is something about you that is so special to me.

I need to go to sleep now. I miss you.

Simone.

Simone's disappointment at John's threesome experience left him confused. Of course there was no emotion. They were just two women wanting to have a good time. In his defence, his treatment of them was gentle, sharing and even humorous at times. His perverse disappointment was also her denial of the possibility of experiencing two men. His disappointment was that she had introduced – dare he think it – a pornographic dimension to the correspondence. Despite his own misgivings (he would never be able to do such a thing himself), he could certainly watch a pornographic simulation of such an event. The interesting thing for him now was, could he sit and watch Simone with two men? Ah! A psychiatrist might have a field day with this.

Meanwhile, she continued to delight in describing the physical side of lovemaking, ensuring of course that it was part of a deeply emotional experience!

May 3.

My dear Simone,

Your gentleness is confounded by falling into despair, followed by the fight to survive and to be strong. Sometimes you manage it and sometimes you feel that you will not make it. It is exhausting. Fear not because at least you have one friend in this world who seems to understand you and desires to comfort, love and protect you within this surreal world of ours. This is amazing, and you are amazing. Loving you in this context seems as natural as waking each morning.

Sweet dreams, gorgeous woman!

John.

May 4.

My sweet darling John,

It is one after midnight... I cannot sleep. I saw your note and it made me feel so warm inside. You are so precious to me. How can I live now without your loving words? I think of you always. I will go to sleep now and dream of you. Cover me with your warm kisses and hold me tight. I need you. I will close my eyes and hold on to you like a child. Kiss me gently between my eyes on my forehead. Tell me that you love me.

Simone.

May 7.

John,

I wonder how your voice sounds. You consume my thoughts all the time. I miss you so much and yearn for your presence. I am so dependent on your e-mails now. I check my inbox a couple of times a day. I wonder how I will cope when you go back home or even when you are on vacation. I understand that you are using global roaming and spending much time on the net; it must be expensive. Do you think you can call me when you get home? Do you think you would want to do so? Would it be okay sometime in future for me to call you? I know that we settled the rules for cyber-relationship boundaries, so I will understand if you preferred to keep it this way.

Simone.

May 7.

Simone,

First, I desired to inhabit nothing but a surreal world of ideas and emotional understanding. I wanted you to mirror the pain of my mother. I wanted to mirror the confusion of your son – both in order to carry ourselves to a level of self-knowledge that would let us cope with our individual pain, and for me, my enduring confusions. You soon sent a photograph and I was amazed by what I saw. Eventually, I relented and sent you a photograph in return. Your reaction was equally profound. Now, secondly, you venture closer to reality. A picture is something but it's still only a picture. Talking is real-time – the here and now. No hiding from that. Will I succumb? I don't know. Reality can be frightening.

John.

May 9.
Sweet darling,

I am so exhilarated by being so close to my freedom. I will never, ever remarry. Marriage is a bondage institution for slow death. I hate it. One of the things I resented the most through our married years was the temperature in our home. I never felt comfortable. It was so cold in the summer and even worse in winter. In bed, I was never warm and he always pushed the covers away. He would refuse to hold me while sleeping! The rationale is that it was uncomfortable. There were so many little stupid things that chipped away at my spirit. I could not be any happier for its coming to an end. I want to take a deep breath and burst with happiness. My only regret is my children. I fully understand that I am putting them in a bad situation. That is the only thing that is painful.

I also thought that after my full separation and a little

time, I would love to see you. It would be great if you could come and stay with me for a few days. God, the mere thought thought is so fascinating. I imagined this afternoon that we were sitting together holding hands and talking. Just that idea filled me with rapture. I can only really imagine how it would feel to be between your arms. I want to let go of all these years of pain between your arms. I want to bury my face in your chest and feel your hands rub my hair as you tell me that it is okay.

Simone.

May 12.

Dear Simone,

The institution of marriage is well intentioned. It provides stability for the resulting children or a lasting bond for two people who simply *know* that they shall be together forever, whether children ensue or not. For mere mortals however, marriage can be fun but it can quickly descend into a struggle – a physical and emotional grind. Sometimes it is neither, just a wasting away of the original spirit that brought the couple together in the first place, because of circumstances they never conceived of ever being inflicted upon them.

A more optimistic notion is one of freedom, to choose how to use it, spend it and waste it, or just to have it. That is selfish in one way but it also heightens the need to understand your own needs as well.

When I travel, it is the only time I have to write and think and dream and drift. This relationship of ours would be unsustainable if I did not travel. Writing erotic imaginings would not be possible without accommodating lounges at airports! It is, though, a very solitary existence. The challenge seems to be how to reconcile the two extremes.

Do you ever think you might find solace, friendship (and even love) in the company of a woman? It might be one way out of the dilemma of maintaining freedom yet having a foundation of companionship.

As for seeing me, heavens, there is no greater reality than that. I fear to even contemplate such a thing. It would be too… sublime.

John.

May 13.

Dear John,

I want to give you something different. I want to wrap you with a blanket of warm loving… pure and unconditional and without any demands or expectations.

Do you fear reality? I do not. I know that when we meet and make love it will be beautiful. We will not be making love really but we will be reaching out to a higher truth – open, naked, honest truth of our frailty and vulnerability. We would give each other warmth that has abandoned our hearts through these long years of isolation. I want to open myself up for you, fully trustingly and innocently. Please take care of me. Shelter me between your arms and I will shelter you. I love you, my sweet angel. Sleep tight and dream of happier days. Meanwhile, think of this.

'You raise yourself up and cover my body.

"Kiss me, John. Tell me that I am very, very beautiful!"

You position yourself between my legs. I am wet, wet, wet. You massage my legs and take one and put it on one shoulder.

"No... No, John!" You smile at me and kiss my knee and lick it a little right there. This brings a surge of tingling all the way down my spine. I relax a little. You pull my other leg. I am resisting. I am afraid that it will hurt. You tell me that it will not. You tell me that I will love it. You push your fullness inside me all at once with controlled force and power. I gasp! I lose my breath and cry with pleasure.

"Yes, yes, it feels wonderful!"

Fill the voids of my spirit, my precious darling. I am all yours. I surrender to your strength. I want you. I want you hard – very, very hard. I feel your power yet I sense your tenderness. A fabulous combination and I trust you. You start slowly pumping me and I stretch the length of my body to meet your strength. You feel me tighten up inside so you pump harder and harder. I writhe with pleasure and pain.

"You are so beautiful!"

The more I tighten up the more you push. You hold my legs even tighter. I try to pull back but you pull me forward and you smile. I find myself returning the smile. You love me again and again and again. I take you into my heart and open it wide. You feel the tingling sensation wrap your mind all the way down your spine. You let go.

"Let go, my love, and take me inside your heart."

We both radiate and shine as our loving energy wraps both our bodies with mist and desire. The moment of our union is suspended in eternity – a fraction of a second where our spirits meet and unite so lovingly. We both come with power and force like we have never experienced before...'

Simone.

May 14.

Darling John,

I want more. I just want to cover you with my loving words. I know this is too much for both of us; I know that. Do you think we are both crazy? I giggle now with anticipation. We have really abandoned all reason and let go of all rationalisation of reality. It is okay my darling! It is all right! I just want to melt and melt again into you in every possible way.

If all I have is e-mail, so be it. Remember that wherever our journey will take us, I will never take you away from your family. I personally plan on never ever getting married. I was stupid once, so there is no reason to be stupid twice.

Simone.

May 15.

My sweet darling John,

My feelings are simply pouring out of me. I cannot describe what I am going through. I really cannot. It is a very virtual inner set of thoughts that are so, so strange. I am sad and happy, lonely and yet have you in my mind as a constant companion; I only wish our connection would last. I fear the hands of time for those are so deceiving.

No, I do not have a female friend who would be a source of solace (or even love) in my life. I am too sensitive to even begin seeking such a thing. It is too difficult and sometimes a thought is better than reality.

I am wondering about your two friends and their rejection that (happily) led you to me. What is it exactly that you asked them to do – the cyber-communication? It cannot be that, surely? What is the role that I am performing in your life? I have very much let go of shaping things between us and I am having a free flow of communication without much inhibition or control. Is that a good thing? I think you did the same thing. Are you going to come to your reality – your senses – and tell yourself that is a crazy thing we have done? What is driving our communication? How did we end up talking at such a level? I smile warmly and think of your e-mails and think that your internal beauty has driven much of my responses. It is a mix of motherly care and now, even at a different level, emotional contact and physical desire. It is a beautiful evolution but it is in the raw and I do not want to shape anything. I want to freely feel you in my life.

Yes, a phone call will make our relationship more realistic. Why are you afraid of that? I think at some time in the future we will have a review of what we are both going through. Meanwhile, let us dance this cosmic connection. Let me teach you how to love and how to feel. Let me hold you in my arms and you will let go all these years of confusion and pain. You have never been loved the way you deserve to be loved! Sex is not love. I hope I can teach you that sex is only a dimension of the loving language.

You think that to connect with a woman you have to use the physical means: that you have to "please" and in return you will be loved! Am I right? That is what I think, so discuss this with me further.

What a horrible thing marriage is. I am dead, dead, dead only in marriage. I cry and cry and cry but there is not much I can do. I just cannot continue this way. I am living a daily hell in knowing that I am not loved. Is this selfishness? I do not know. I have got to run now. I look forward to reading your next instalment. Stay with me, John. I do not know if I can give you much more beyond words. I know words at some point are not the same as the real physical touch. I am here today and want to stay for a long time in your life.

Simone.

John,

I would love so much to hear your voice. I can only imagine how you sound.

Simone.

15.

May 17.

Dear John,

I have been depressed over the past two days. I silently weep and see no comfort in sight. Tomorrow, my husband is leaving for a five day trip to his family in another state. He will take my son with him. I watched my son all night – every move, every smile, every word. I held him in my arms for a half hour. I could hear his heartbeat. I feel so helpless and wonder if he will ever forgive me. Despair and darkness is all I feel.

I saw my lawyer today and finalised the separation agreement. Next week, we will both sign it and, with that, ten years of my life will come to an end. What a mix of feelings. Here is a scenario that is recurrent in my conversations with my husband. He says, "You have no heart! You will regret your decision and will know that you fucked up and by then it will be too late."

My heart sinks deeper into a dark hole and I feel nothing. I am very numb and say, "To hell with you! I cannot wait to see the end of this stupid marriage." The irony is that I know for sure that he does not love me but the comfort of being married appeals to him. He does not want to stay in this marriage because I mean nothing but a blanket of comfort, a convenience! That is what I have been over the past years. Even sexually, I am nothing but convenience. I know I am not perfect and I have done my share to ruin this marriage, but deep inside, I feel depressed. What the future holds for me I can only wonder. I read, a long time ago, that when humans go to war or face extremely stressful situations like death, divorce or unemployment, the body triggers internal self-defence mechanisms. Depression and weeping are defence mechanisms to release grief. Having an affair is also an internal mechanism. You and I are like two leafs tossed in the wind. We are aimlessly floating on the currents of the wind. Circling and circling with no relief in sight. What will happen when we hit the ground?

What were you thinking when you looked at my pictures? It is rather strange, the whole connection; it is almost surreal.

You know that I attempted suicide when I was eighteen in response to my lover's rejection of me. Needless to say I survived but my life was never the same after that. I still reach inside myself where I curl and close my eyes, wishing to not ever wake up again. What a shame!

Deep inside I am haunted with memories of the past. It feels like a cobweb in my mind. I cannot describe the haunting despair a person feels when life loses its meaning to a point where one seeks an end. WHY WAS I NOT LOVED THEN? WHY I AM I NOT LOVED NOW? WHY THE PAIN? WHY? I do not think that I will ever be loved. I am sorry. Tonight, my heart is heavy.

Simone.

May 18.
Simone,

You are suffering badly. I'm so sorry! You must cry till the tears dry up. Then you must gather your strength. You must fight all this pain because you have such a future, full of choice and prospect. You just can't see it now. Close your emotional system down for a week or two while the papers go through (will the official separation agreement, then divorce, be over quickly?). Look upon it as the instrument of your freedom. Once you achieve that freedom, the world will be yours! So don't worry about notions of comforting and loving me to provide solace in an emotionally crazy world. For now it is you that needs all the help and all the words of love and support. I looked at your pictures, yes. I just stared at them and tried to look deep, deep into you and to feel you and hear your breathing and wondered if that is as close as I may ever get to you (which might be the case). If so, I must be strong and simply make sure you get back on track to, eventually, find some happiness.

Simone! What you clearly don't see in your world just now is that you have so much to offer professionally and personally. You've already told me about how senior managers look at you at work longingly and that you resist such things, seeking to get on in your career on merit. That is an admirable position and you must stick to it! On the personal side, things are different. Once your pain subsides (and it will), you shall start feeling good and strong. Being young, you will start feeling frisky, needing both love and eventually release (or maybe the other way around). The point is that you will not be short of suitors and ultimately one will appear who might fulfil both your emotional and erotic desires. However, you must make your needs plain to him. You must also make it clear that marriage is not an option (though in time you might relent). Even if the scenario does not form in that way, the essential truth will be that (a) your grief will abate, (b) your freedom will be granted, (c) you will be pursued and therefore (d) you will be able to pick and choose who to love and when!

My dear, having choices is having power! It is the richest freedom of all. I have none. You have many choices and therefore much power! There is no doubt that you will have many offers of love (and many of just sheer lust). Most of all, you will have the option of love. My only regret now is that I cannot provide you with that emotional AND sensual love. Talking (I mean writing, of course) with you on such things is beautiful but it is not the same as being and doing! I have spent the last week painfully adjusting to that inevitable truth. As for suicide, the difference between you and me is you attempted it. I calculated it as a rational option in my late twenties (when I had failed, yet again, to find love). I was devastated and alone, yet I got through it in my own way, with no help. For fear of repeating myself, my May 21st advertisement was my first open cry for help! You responded and for that, and for knowing you and for bringing me to this point, you will always be in my heart.

For the immediate… we must get you through this awful patch. I am with you.

John.

May 18.

My sweet darling John,

Your words are soothing and healing. I have calmed down a lot emotionally. Today is the first day without my husband and son. Last night, I freaked out as I waited for my husband to call me and let me know that the trip was okay and they are fine. It was nine in the evening before I was fed up and I looked for his family's number in an old phone bill and called. I did not make much of a scene. I hid my anger and talked pleasantly to all of them and asked to talk to my son. He came, talked about the police car and the nearby firehouse and how happy he is. He innocently told me that he will be back soon. Then he left. All together the call lasted five minutes – such pain I feel, such awful pain!

I feel tears while remembering the start of my marriage. I was totally in love. However, I started to notice awkward things starting from our wedding night. Even then, things began to change. Our honeymoon was a disaster. I will stop here and continue later. I should write a book.

Simone.

16.

May 21.

My sweet darling,

I am still vibrating with happiness and disbelief. Did we just talk today or was it my imagination… my God! I am falling in love with you. I am so happy. Your voice is like music. It vibrates directly through to my heart. I just loved hearing you talk. It is astounding, so marvellous. I have not felt this happy in a long time. Your voice is so soothing. When you call my name, my heart just beats with joy. Oh, John, I now understand your disbelief. Your accent is delicious. The way you utter words is beyond electrifying. When you said the word "together" I just felt dizzy! John, John, John… I can call your name forever. My sweet darling John. The way you express yourself is so wonderful.

I am sure the minute we meet, bolts of thunder and lightning will erupt in our hearts. My knees were so weak when I heard your voice and my joy was unprecedented. Yes, it is very emotional but so wonderful. I close my eyes now and think of you sleeping in your spacious hotel bed. How do you sleep, John? On your back? On your side?

Which side: left or right? Do you curl yourself into a foetal position? I sleep on my back and raise my arm and cover my my eyes, then I toss and turn on my sides. The covers have to be all the way up, covering my shoulders, otherwise I will not be able to sleep.

John! Was the reality of my voice a scary thing for you? I thought that the reality of your voice is the most precious gift I have ever been given. You give me life and hope! Do you know that? You lift me up from despair and open windows of light into the darkness of my heart. Your sunshine dries my tears and makes me whole again. Yes, I will see you one day. Yes, one day I will be one with you. We will both know the ultimate unity of our spirits. I do not fear that day. I yearn and long for that day. It will be just as mystical and wonderful as today. I just cannot get over the beauty of your voice. It still resonates inside my heart.

I can only imagine the beauty of touching you for real! I was so dizzy today as you told me that you were full of desire for me. Hearing your voice calling my name is beyond my ability to describe. I can tell you that I am glowing, literally glowing, with happiness. For now, I just want to close my eyes and enjoy feeling you again inside me. I just want to replay your words in my mind over and over again.

John! Are you as happy as I am?
Simone.

May 21.
Dearest Angel,
In our phone call, from which I am still reeling, you asked

me about a specific favourite position? This is a very difficult question! However, I think that I like it best when we are facing each other. You are sitting. I am sitting in your lap, facing you, my legs wrapped around your waist, my hands around your neck, your manhood deep inside me. I would like for us to kiss and our tongues to meet while we are both fully embracing each other, my breasts against your chest, brushing you as I rise and slide down. I think that I would like this best. I love it because I hang on to you with my arms, yet I feel you inside and my legs are wrapped around you and we can still kiss each other and say soft sweet things to each other. This is a sacred tantric position as well. I cannot recall the name but it is by far my favourite.

Simone.

May 22.

My beautiful Simone,

I interchange between your picture on my screen and a black and white paper version, just printed. I retain your gentle voice in my head. I put both together with your words and I have a heady concoction evoking warmth and desire, love and passion, controlled and sustained penetration. How will I survive such joy? I sleep on my right side; I curl up, sometimes into a little ball, like an infant. Covers must cover right up to my ear, even in a warm place. I wake up feeling drowsy and looking like a mess. I creep into the bathroom and shower, feeling the soothing warm jet bringing me back to life and the semblance of a normal appearance. I shave later. Breakfast is simple, percolated coffee and toast. Once consumed, I can take on the world (for the next couple of hours anyway).

One glorious day perhaps, we might dance together. The reality of your voice was a bolt of lightning but with such gentleness. I must get used to the reality of meeting the real you in real time. I am more than one person. I think of domestic realities and seek to make that as good as possible for all concerned. I am also a person away from home: one who dreams and explores ideas, who thinks (and now) dreams and loves through space. I wanted to repeat everything you said just to increase the pleasure of you. Is this a scary notion? I hope I will experience the whole range of experiences with you. I want to know you when you are sad so that I can comfort you, and when you are happy so that I can share in your joy of life again.

You are so perfectly lovely. I just do not know how this has come about. I do not deny it; I never deny it. It is a new dimension to my life and one I hope will endure and even enrich my life at home. You seem like vulnerable perfection. I want to protect and love you and hear your voice again and again and again. In my heart and my spirit, you know I am yours. Why is a grown man like me saying such a thing? Yet I am and I do with total conviction.

I can just feel you sitting in my lap with your thighs apart, devoted to my penetration. You move yourself up and down my strength and hardness from time to time as we maintain our embrace. We talk gently and whisper softly of love and eternal devotion. I feel the fullness of your breasts against my chest. I bend down from time to time and try to kiss them, then return to your face, your eyes and your mouth. What love this is.

Stay strong, my beauty. I am with you.

John.

May 24.

My sweet darling,

I feel like a teenager! I am falling in love with you, Johnnnnnnnnnnnnnnnnnnnnnn!!! It is so crazy but I am happy.

Darling, I will be online today at two p.m. my time. What time is that for you? Your voice is still resonating inside my heart. I just cannot believe this! I had a silly dream that one day I would take you to Spain. I would walk you through the steps of El Cid. Just a thought: a far-fetched thought but it was delicious to imagine such a thing. I have to run now. I will be back in two hours. I hope you are there. I love you. I love you. I love you.

Simone.

May 25.

My sweet darling,

I am very free in my spirit and mind and body but I do not flaunt myself. I am a lady in the very classical sense and do carry myself in public with much decorum. I am experiencing liberation of my sexuality with you. I am opening my spirit to be free. My feelings for you are transcendental in nature. I just cannot explain.

When I told you that I am falling in love, it is beautiful. It is not a reason to worry about me getting hurt. No. It is different kind of love, you must admit. Not a regular relationship and so forth. I also understand that this was like a honeymoon. You will not be able to write to me as you did in the past few weeks. I understand, my love – honestly! I am mature enough to understand where our connection resides (in the heart). Our medium of communication may become severely restricted. Sadly, that is reality. In the meantime, your love is in my heart and will blossom and flourish.

No matter what happens, John, I will always love you. Even if for some mad reason I end up losing my connection with you, the reality is I love you. That will not change or be touched. You gave me much peace and comfort over the past days, and for that I am grateful. I dared to talk to you twice. Maybe it was a stupid thing to do but that is okay. I relished having heard your voice. Now when I read your words, I can hear your voice and with your picture, you really come through the pages – alive! Maybe that is as close as we can get. It is perfectly all right to me. With that said, I must stop, my sweet darling angel.

Simone.

17.

May 28.

My angel Simone,

Already, today has been a much busier day, so I have had less time tonight. It is also a premonition of things to come. I feel sad that I am going to lose this brief freedom that has turned a possible twenty-one days of absence into a serious outpouring of unfolding emotion. For me it has been a devastating experience, revealing myself to be an emotional being after all and with all the shafts of insight that flow from it. My sadness is for selfish reasons. At the end of each day, I have normally managed to unwind with a gracefully energetic run. I have then joined my colleague (a nice person) for a drink before dinner. We have then retreated to our rooms, where I have entered into my fantastic world through this medium and into you. I have been able to do it virtually at leisure and when I felt able and emotionally ready. I have not had to snatch at time so that I can fire off some little message to you.

Anyway, that is why I feel sad now. You write with such maturity of our love and the fact that we do not inhabit a real world. Honeymoon? What a delightful way of putting it; you are right! It has been a blossoming sensation. I remain stunned at my own response and my own desire and my own willingness to open myself up to such things. I love you unashamedly and find myself at a loss as to how to cope without you as intensely as we have recently become. I need your friendship too, of course, and I want to be here when you are low again, as you will be, with those black moods of yours. They are to be banished. If they come to you, think of a Steve Martin movie. Think of anything. Think of the last time you made love and enjoyed it. Just try not to get sucked into that awful feeling of total despair. You are too precious and too lovely for such things. And anyway, your voice makes me melt! I don't know what else to say tonight except that I've been playing classical music on the radio (melancholy!) and think of you constantly.

My love to you.

John.

May 29.

My angel Simone,

You should be blissfully asleep just now (it is almost two a.m. your time). I write simply to welcome you to your Fourth of July celebration. I yearn for your touch and your delicate word. I yearn for my eyelids to be kissed and for my hand to be held. I yearn for your smile and your embrace. You are beauty in my eyes and in my heart.

P.S. Tell me when you feel like being taken by an upright lion – standing, tied and in theory at least, helpless. I'm not sure if this is right but my imagination has run wild. You are tapping deeper into a seam of consciousness that I never knew I had. If I am straying because of a naïve interpretation of the forces you are unleashing in me then help me to channel them in the ways that will bring us enduring unity. Help me!

John.

The lion business was the underlying theme of their second telephone conversation. Her confidence and adventure – the experimentation even – had moved to a point when she was overt about her desire 'to be taken against my will'. What was John to do? Deny the request? How could he? He was besotted by this woman and her ideas, no matter how disturbing to him initially – the two women scene, hardly; the two men possibility, certainly. A dark side was being introduced. In his more rational moments, he realised that something was indeed being uncovered within his psyche. If he was apprehensive, she was not...

May 30.

John,

'I wake up to find myself in a partly dark room. I am disoriented a bit as I find myself standing with my eyes blindfolded, my hands tied to a pole above my head, as if I am suspended helplessly by my hands. It is really quiet but for the sounds of birds and crickets... sounds that I never heard before. I can partially see through my blindfold that I am barefoot but for my anklets and when I move my feet their silver bells make sounds. I see lockets of my black braided hair reaching all the way to my waist, adorned with beads of silver and gold. I regain consciousness. consciousness. I remember a raid in the darkness. I wonder where my servants are, where my guards are, how did this happen? I shake my head to remove the blindfold but can only partially do so. I look at the floor of the room: sapphire blue shades with lotus flowers and hieroglyphic symbols painted all around the pole, with gold and silver rims of beauty. The smell of incense overpowers my senses. I understand that I am taken captive by the Egyptian Pharaoh's army. I am so overpowered by feelings of despair, still tied to the pole and tired. I throw my head forward and tears run down my cheeks... At this point, I hear the footsteps of someone walking very slowly towards me in the room. I stop and my body freezes in fear...'

Now, it is your turn, my love, to finish my fantasy! No, I do not want to restrain us but to celebrate us. Open yourself up to me, my angel, and liberate your most hidden desires. It is beautiful, really. I can only imagine the mix of domination and gentleness in your powerful touch. I have never, never experienced this before. I want to be free with you. I want to feel your control and restraint and to be fully taken by you. The beauty of it is like role-playing, to experience many, many levels of subconsciousness that neither one of us reached before nor knew existed. What a delicious fantasy for me to be tied (I actually find this most erotic) and so helpless. Yet it is deceiving really, as my vulnerability is my strength and the same for you; your strength is really your vulnerability. Yes, we are both experiencing the paranormal, my love, so there is no reason to restrain your desires or thought. We can cross time and space not only in the present but in the past, over thousands and thousands of years. Awaken your mind, my My happiness stems from the fact I can open up in full trust in you that you will treasure my willingness to experience such things with you. At the same time, it will not debase either you or me... so pick up where I left off, my love, and tell me who was it in the room and why.

Simone.

John was still unconvinced about Simone's ultimate denial of the two-male threesome; it was her idea after all! Now, she had moved some considerable steps forward to realms of bondage, domination, sadism and masochism. Looking at her key phrases again for reassurance: 'I do not want to restrain us but to celebrate us... liberate your most hidden desires... domination... and gentleness in your powerful touch. I have never, never experienced this before. I want to be free with you. I to be fully taken by you.' This was certainly 'conquest'. Though in the most explicit and openly acknowledged role playing context, this was a 'rape fantasy'. John had heard, very occasionally, that all women, at one time or another, had a rape fantasy. Whether a spurious concept or not, this was certainly the case here. She wanted it, she was yearning for it. More crudely, she was 'begging for it', a squalid justification in a less enlightened context. What was he to do? He must attempt to fulfil her desire, her fantasy.

June 1.
Simone,
'I am breathing with tiredness because I have been away in the heat and the dust. I ask a retainer about the woman

tied to the post. The servant tells me the woman was captured but that no one has defiled her because of my orders. My blood is racing from the thrill of battle but I am tired. I am tired but I walk around you slowly. I like what I see; the curve of the breasts and the shape of the body. I take my sword and lift what passes for a dress. There is nothing underneath. Your pubic bush is apparent. I let the dress go and ask where you are from. You mutter something then whimper a little. I take my sword again and let it caress your curves, to sense the sensitivity of your skin. You breathe in sharply. By now a servant has brought me a goblet of wine. Water is also there. I hold the water to your lips. You are still tied up. The blindfold remains on. You can see just a little. I see your tongue moving in the water to soothe yourself. My wine and the colour of your tongue suddenly blind me with desire. I take off my outer robe and rip your dress off. You scream. I ignore this. I pause and inspect this gift from my soldiers – this unblemished peach, this picture of loveliness. But desire overtakes such transient thoughts and as you struggle, I take your face in my hand and plunge my tongue into your mouth. You try and resist then realise you can't but don't really want to. You just fear pain. I lower myself and with my unshaved face scratch your breasts as I move there. I take your nipples and suck hard. You scream with fright more than pain. You are crying with fear. I say nothing. I move your legs apart and, with force, enter your secret place. You scream again. I begin. I move, like a great general should. I take you like a lion. I make each thrust count. You almost faint from the mixture of fear and pleasure. You begin to come. I begin to surge. You come and scream out. I roar like a lion as my life pours into you. For the moment it is over.

I recover quickly and look at your forlorn and tired frame drooping with weariness, sobbing quietly. I gather my sword and cut the ropes to free your arms. I remove your blindfold. You look at me with terrified eyes. I signal to you that you will be safe. I call for Leyla. She is my trusted slave; she is very beautiful.

"Leyla, take care of this woman. Clean and prepare her for me. I shall join you presently."

I go off and strip my body of all its war-torn effort. My tub is ready as is always the case. I have a perverse pleasure in washing myself. I lie there, thinking of this woman I have just had... Leyla takes you into another part of the house. There is a deep bath with cool water. The air is hot and so you are glad of it. You hesitate for fear of something happening to you. Leyla assures you nothing will. You sink into the pool and feel the water stinging your wrists where you were tied for so long. She sees this and starts to prepare some lotion. You stay in the pool until you feel cleansed and healed. Fresh water is brought for you to drink. Fruit, cheese and figs appear as if from nowhere. You are beckoned out of the water. A towel is offered. You are moved to a couch. You are told to lie down. It is hot but a gentle breeze flows by. The towel is removed by Leyla. She reveals your beauty. She has her lotion and starts to massage your wrists. They feel immediately healed. She moves up your arm and then down the other. She touches your forehead and your cheeks and laughs playfully. She pours oil on your breasts and starts to massage, one hand on each, touching and checking that your nipples become erect. She stoops to kiss each one. You feel scared but excited. She massages each entire breast until they are soothed. She moves to the legs, then back up. She eases your your legs apart and massages your pussy till it begins to respond. She kisses you there and has a little flick with her tongue. You feel less scared. You are asked to turn over. Your back is gently caressed. Your legs are taken one by one and rubbed slowly. You feel whole again and rested and sleepy. Your eyes close and you dream of the man who has just taken you.

You wake from you slumber to find that unbeknown to you, the hands of a woman have become the hands of a man, a glistening, strong man wearing just a loin cloth. You look aghast, fearing for more of the harsher side of passion.

I leave you on your front and take my loincloth off, give it to Leyla and signal to her to stay. I touch you all over and kiss both ears as a prelude. I move to your legs and pull them apart. There is no sentiment. I reveal the delicious sight of your pussy, already glistening with moisture. Your legs stretch as wide apart as I can spread them. I kiss you there and kiss the wetness too. I taste you and feel you respond to my tongue's deep penetration. I am erect and wanting you again. I climb on top and prepare myself for entry. You hold your breath, not believing the possibility of gentleness. There is none. I plunge into you, as far as I can go. I stay deep, deep down, then start pumping. Your body is trembling with excitement or fear, I'm not sure which. I move into an almost vicious mode, fucking this prisoner as hard as I can. While pumping, Leyla is stroking my balls as she often does; this time her own cunt is not needed. I explode with my ejaculation – one of the advantages of a woman's manipulation of my balls. I retain enough power to get you to come, you doing so against your obvious will; you were trying to resist. Your scream was a mixture of resentment – hatred even – and pain; the denial pleasure was, however, impossible to disguise. I become completely sentimental.

"Be mine, my love," I say. You move your head a round, not believing what you are hearing. You see the tears in my eyes. I have found love. I have really found love. I take one leg of yours and wrap it around my head so that you can turn over. You do so with my manhood still inside you. I rest you down again and lie on you.

"Will you love me? Will you love me forever? Please will you love me forever?" As I plead, the gentle surges of joy start to unfold yet again. My body arches in spasms to magnify the joy. You move and groan and scream with ecstasy. We are spent but it is not over. With our nakedness, we cling together. I pick you up and carry you to the bed chamber. We enter and Leyla closes the door behind her. We are quite alone. I place you on the bed and ask if you will love me forever and be only mine. You smile and take my hand in affirmation. I am full of joy and apology for the earlier scene. You touch my brow and lay my head to rest. You turn me to my right side and cuddle yourself into the back of my shape. You stroke my back and my neck. Already I am sleeping, knowing I have found my one true love.'

John.

18.

June 4.
Dear Simone,

It's 1.42 p.m. I have been home twenty-three hours. I arrived at Heathrow to a smiling wife and two adoring children. Much hugging and kissing and chattering ensued. There is always a little friction between Heather and I on my return. It is simply the work-thing when abroad – very dynamic and intense, impacting on a more modest domestic reality. It settles within a day. As I felt myself tiring that evening, I thought of our messages and how important they are and how they can carry me back to how I should be permanently; a positive dynamic and imaginative individual!

By eight p.m. I turn to her and declare exhaustion. She is displeased. I apologise and go straight to bed. I wake up eleven hours later! Physically I'm fine but I miss you. The household wakes up at different times – the children are on their summer vacation now – no school till September. Breakfasts are consumed, and by nine thirty a.m. our aging Volvo carries three children and two adults to the local sports centre. It's swimming lesson time; we watch, contentedly.

Our evening meal is now finished; 6.34 p.m. It is the

one time we are all at the one place together. We try and instil basic manners and courtesies. Sometimes it works but it's just nice to be together, with the TV off, just talking for a little while as one unit. Then people disperse for their long summer evening activities – and that, I think, is the last of domestic reality.

So, I fight to retain my spirit for, in my opinion, the higher things of life. I, therefore, write and share, often with passion, with sensuality and sometimes with just raw sex, with you. Please stay with me! Please reflect on what we have achieved so far. Please tell me and reassure me of everything.

John.

June 5.

Dear sweet angel John,

Yes, I did much reflection over our conversations and e-mails over the past few weeks. I am happy with your presence in my life. I am thrilled and amused at our communications. How on earth did we reach such a state? You are so special and so wonderful. Everything about you is just right. I marvel at the way you express yourself and the dynamics of our exchange. It is surely fundamental to me to have you in my life. You are like my guardian angel. I think of you so much. When I face certain situations I wonder how you would respond. You are so mature and experienced both emotionally and professionally.

John, I asked before and you either did not want to answer or missed my question. I will ask again and if you do not want to answer, I will respect your choice. Why do you have such a rift between you and your wife in terms of intimacy? It also seems that it is you who is not making the initiative. Do you understand your inhibition or lack of willingness to engage her with your love? As I said before, after the birth of my son, I just could not bear the thought of being touched at all. It was even physically painful. I refused it altogether for a year. Things changed over time but in my heart is not the same.

I will send you my re-draft of The General this weekend.

Today, I am in the office. It has been a long, tiring day. In your relationship with Heather, put effort in reaching out to her. She loves you. Just think, John, you are a lucky man! Two women love you and they are much younger than you are. You must be doing something right. I will not leave you, my darling angel. I am here and will always be here. I hold you at night as I too curl into a ball.

Simone.

June 8.

Darling Simone,

Recapture your spiritual energy and beauty before committing more to paper. Be at peace and be strong, my love, for I surely need it! I miss you and your thoughts even for these fleeting absences but I know that my bond with you and my love for you grows stronger and stronger. Is that possible? The answer is that this relationship knows no bounds. "Is it right?" you ask. "It surely is!" you answer. How right you are! I love you (and, yes, I loved our conversation before I finally left New Delhi). What a revelation you are to me and what a revelation I am to myself – surprises all around I think.

I write like this and feel immediately taken from the domestic world I inhabit. What a mental, and indeed emotional, release. You succour me (let alone offer the potential to suckle me, but that's for another time again). So, please do: tell me where I went wrong in The General and what you would have wanted. Then perhaps you can tell me how I can sustain your love for me and how I can support you in other matters too.

I love you very much, Simone. Your words bring me such pleasure and emotional comfort. I hope you are well.

John.

June 9.

Dear, dear John,

Tell me where I went wrong in The General? You did not go wrong in The General; it was delightful. However, I did expect more force in taking me. You did not provide that forceful verbal and physical description in detail. I thought you were a little genteel or concerned to reveal such behaviour. As my shock evaporated when you first asked me to be your "whore", I started to feel somewhat aroused at the thought and expected maybe some revelation towards such a request – especially when you described a scenario where you would love to take me while tied up...

Yes, while bits of the conquest were rough, the ending

was indeed 'genteel' if not simply gentle. John hesitated. He did not fully comprehend the depths of Simone's hunger. He He was afraid to 'let go'. In truth, he had never 'let go' in such a way. This was entirely new to both his thinking and even his level of desire. New aspects within him were being tapped into – his latent dark side perhaps. Yet, it was Simone's dark side that was the focus of her own hunger – the desire to be conquered, to be treated like a whore. Interesting!

Here is a re-draft, if you will, of The General... not to say that I did not enjoy your version – it was lovely, so lovely – but here is my desire for another possible scenario:

'My head hurts as I shake it, gently trying to get rid of this blindfold. I can partially see some light and hear some noise outside. These cursed Egyptians! They will pay for their foolishness! How dare they take me a hostage! I am angry yet afraid. I feel the soreness of my hands and wrists as I stand tied up to a pole. My hands are above my head supporting my drooping body. I am blindfolded.

I hear a man's voice. He is asking about me. His voice is deep and powerful. The slave murmurs a few words as he slams the door. He is angry or in a bad mood. I freeze my body, not making a sound. I wish to vanish. I hear his footsteps as he circles me. I sense what he is contemplating and my heart fills with anxiety, yet deep inside I am thrilled. I tell myself that I must fight him, yet I know inside that I do not want to.

His hand reaches my cheeks. His fingers pull open my lips. With his hand, he massages my lips forcefully, brings himself closer. I pull my head and body back as far as I can, but he pins me against the pole with one hand as he pulls my face towards him. I scream, asking him to leave me alone. He lunges his tongue into my mouth. The taste of his lips is absolutely overpowering as he darts his tongue in and out.

I lose my balance. I almost slip. He holds me by my waist. He pulls my blindfold off. My long black lashes open up, showing him my deep dark brown eyes glistening with fear and anger. I command him to let me go. He laughs as he holds my lips with his hand, so I bite him with full force. He pulls his hand back and his laughter turns to anger as he sees that I drew blood. He pulls my head back by my hair and dives his head to the nape of my neck and tells me I will regret what I did.

I break down trembling with fear. I cry and my tears fill my eyes. He holds my dress between his hands, tears it apart and partially slides it down my shoulders as he pins me against the pole. I start kicking and writhing my body under his while he plunges his mouth into my shoulders. I struggle as he kisses and licks my neck and shoulders, and he slathers me with his lashing tongue. I cry. I cry with fear and joy.

In one move, he pulls my dress down to my waist. His hands move to my breasts. He squeezes them as he moves down, scratching the softness of my skin with his rough face. So much pain and so much pleasure overtake my body. I start dripping and feel my wetness overcome me. He pulls my dress with savage force as he finds his way into my pussy. I scream with horror.

"No, no, *no*. . . Please stop!"

He does not listen as he thrusts his tongue inside me. I moan with fear and pleasure and surge into spasms of orgasms. He can feel me tighten up and tastes the release of my juices on his tongue.

He stands up and admires my nakedness. He is still clothed. He asks, "Did you like that, you little whore?" I do not answer and cry a little. He tells me to answer him. I venture to answer but he screams again as his anger starts to well up again. I answer with mixed tears.

"*Yes! Yes!* I liked it!"

As I answer, he pulls his robes open. I gasp! He is fully erect. His body is supremely beautiful. I pull my legs together for fear of what is to come. He notices and gets angrier. He commands me: "Spread your legs now, you fucking whore! How dare you pull them together in front of me!"

I pull them together harder. He plunges into me as he pulls my legs apart with frenzied madness.

I scream with horror. I kick. I fight. He does not listen. He opens my legs wide with his forceful hands and plunges his hard cock into me with power, harder and harder. My screams drown and subside with trembling moans as my body starts to enjoy his thrusting, hard cock.

"Ohh!" I moan.

He whispers into my ear. "Yes, my whore, enjoy me. Take me in, you little fucking bitch."

I moan further and further and I cry with pleasure as my

body tenses with desire and my muscles spasm with orgasm again and again.

I am coming. My body starts pulsating but he does not stop. He pushes harder, driving me crazy with pleasure. I moan and moan as I feel the wonders of my femininity surge and drip my wetness on to him. I come again and again. He slows down as he surges inside me.

"My beautiful fucking whore," he says as he comes deep inside me. His breathing is rough with pleasure. He reaches to my ropes, cuts me loose and holds me tight, kissing me.

"You sweet, beautiful whore," he tells me as he and I fully embrace. We feel the surging energy of almost bestial desire.

Simone.

She had now committed herself to the idea and the fictional reality of being taken against her will – by force – and enjoying it, her rape fantasy being described with no ambiguity, and frankly, without prompting. She was dissatisfied with his relatively tame original. Whether latent or not, she was now relishing the dark side of her sexuality. One could argue that John had done her a service – that there was therapeutic value in their sharing of ideas, initially emotional and maternal, and now this other deeply sensual stuff. Admittedly, the idea was in the context of John being the conqueror. Yet it still left something unanswered. His problem was that he couldn't quite put this thought into words. He supposed it came down to the 'two women' thing (still harmless) or the 'two men' option (still disturbing). What was his way of thinking though? Surely it wasn't that word again – jealousy? Surely not that! For heaven's sake, what right had he to be jealous? What reason, even?

The contradiction was – and it may be widespread, the utterly selfish side of the male ego – that he would enjoy and participate again if the opportunity presented itself – in a threesome, him and two women. Why then was the idea of him with a suitable male partner fucking a woman so hostile to his thoughts? He supposed that it could only be that he was not a homosexual or bisexual person. A Freudian would no doubt offer a candid and plausible explanation. In any case, this was an interesting development. Simone had become hot and, some would say, pornographic. John had never bothered with porn before – maybe now he would start. From his perspective, his appetite had been whetted. There was no turning back. The question was which way forward was he going to travel. Where was this exploration taking him?

19.

June 14.

Dear John,

I need some time to go into my shell and contemplate my life and where things are headed and how it will all turn out, especially financially. I have no idea yet how my financial affairs should be arranged, so I need to focus. I am not worried about my solvency but the technical arrangements and paying of bills; all this I have never done before. I start school on September 1st, so there is much to do and to manage. Today, I do not have much planned. I think I am coming down with flu and my whole body is very tense. I will go now and take a long, warm shower. Last night, I was shivering with fever. My mother is taking such good care of me. That is so wonderful. My husband and I discussed this ugliness we inflicted upon each other and decided that we want to stay good friends so no more fighting. I truly hope that this is the case.

I re-read my draft of The General! I am so shocked at myself and feel so strange at these descriptions. I would have never expressed such things in a million years, yet they feel delicious and wonderful. Tell me about your impressions when you read it. I was worried a little today that I am breaking every rule of decorum and good manners! I am in reality such a good girl. If you were to meet me, I am such a well-mannered woman. I do not feel in the least that what we exchange is shameful. Actually it is exhilarating. I just love it with much childish thrills.

Simone.

June 15.
Simone,

Your version of The General was luscious and perfect; good girl! No! In fact, it was much, much more than that. It revealed a depth of dark, erotic passion in you that yearns to see and feel the darkness of night descend and consume you. Maybe one day I shall be that darkness. Now, *I* reflect on how on earth I am writing such things; yet I am! What are we doing to each other? What are we discovering in each other? Only time will tell.

John.

At least now, they had both recognised that they had tapped into the dark side of erotic experience. Arguably, this characteristic is, potentially at least, in all of us. The puritanical would shrill in their horror of such a possibility. Yet, John had uncovered something within himself and Simone was responding with gusto. It was exhilarating! He had to write again.

June 16.
Darling Simone,

Such savage beauty you describe in The General. Such evocation of lust and desire. Such explicit wanting by you the man of your dreams. I can hardly bear to think of it. It is almost overpowering. How can you write with such desire, so erotically. How have we come so far, my love? I drafted the original General last week and as you say, you could tell I hesitated. Even then, I was nervous about how far I was permitted to go and, indeed, how far I even wanted to. I might try again. For now though, I want to dwell on the simple idea of love and how it is going to sustain us (do you think it really will?).

I fear sometimes that our distance and your physical reality will be too much to cope with as you are tossed and turned by the vagaries of this practical world we inhabit. The next three months are going to be tough on you but your plans seem very positive, which is so good – July preparing; August, the dreadful month; September, recovery. Who knows, maybe sometime then or after I shall slip across the ocean and make love to you with such beauty and delicacy (the first time), such adventure (the second), and with awesome force (the third) that your head and heart will spin with pure, pure love for your spiritual connection somewhere over the sea.

My love to you.

John.

June 20.

My sweet darling John,

You wonder about the vagaries of the basic realities of

our world. I thought a lot about your question. Is it really the close encapsulation of time and space that preserves a relationship? Here I am after eleven years of shared time and space. Did it help preserve my love? I go even further back to fifteen years ago, and again, what I thought was my first and true love becomes a physical time and space presence. Did it preserve my love? No. Time, space, and closeness do not really guarantee the survival of love. Of course, I am not debating that that closeness is much more powerful than a long distance relationship. Yet the mere presence of closeness does not preserve love. What does? To me it is the essential and genuine caring about each other. Everything else is a manifestation of such care. Think about fire: it glows, it is warm, but what is at the core of fire is the total passionate embrace of energy. Everything else is a manifestation of this energy. I believe in marriage or human relationships – the manifestation of this energy – is love, which fades once this energy fades; it is no longer nourished.

Do you sustain me? Yes. Over the past weeks I have found much hope and much strength in talking to you. No matter what happens in the future, I am sustained and happy because of you. Do I wonder about if it will last? Not really. I am so happy with your presence in my life. You are such a kindred spirit, my love. I ache to hold you and show you my love. Yes, I am very passionate but I am very romantic as well. How was I able to express myself in such manner to you? I do not know, honestly! I let myself flow with wind and water and just be free. I expressed my total desire to be consumed by you, to be ravaged and taken so wonderfully and forcefully by you. Such expression satisfies a basic need that I never foresaw in myself before. I am thrilled that I can be who I am with you. I do want to be with you, with no boundaries and no limits. I just want to melt with you emotionally and spiritually and physically. I want to interchange between all these levels, all at the same time. I want to love you emotionally, feel your gentle touch and loving care. I want to share a spiritual connection of harmony and enlightenment with you. And yes, I do want to share the most expressive physical rawness with you. Just like the sea – sometimes gentle and breezy, sometimes forceful and daring, like nature in all its beauty and savagery, yet all of it as an essential expression of our energy. My love to you.

Simone.

June 21.

Simone,

I weep with love and tenderness. You are so pure and so passionate and so all consuming. I cannot begin to match your heightened emotions but at some point soon, I shall try, especially as a farewell message, before my two-week holiday, when such a message will have to sustain you until my return. Meanwhile, my love, a rougher encounter is brewing in my mind. It needs to be polished for maximum pleasure and thrills on both our parts. More later, though not too far away I hope. I love you dearly and I understand the spiritual completeness of our bond. You are truly a marvel and a revelation and I love you so!

John.

June 21.

John,

I will follow up tomorrow with a detailed e-mail but now I need to go home. I am working late and getting tired. I want to give you a big hug.

Simone.

20.

June 25.

Simone,

By the end of this week I shall be meeting you on The Plane (a return to the central me). You have encouraged me to dominate you (The General was too tame – you wanted more and wrote of such things).

I thrill at your voice and want to hear it constantly, yet know that such abandonment can do me no ultimate good. I am naive and silly. I just believe in you as an idea as well as a person and find that dependence scary for I have never let myself believe in anyone – ANYONE (even today). My first belief remains myself. If I become weak and dependent, I lose what control I have (which is, already, little). Help me, Simone! I need your insight and support. In truth I need what I dare not ask for. I need your love! My heart goes out to you.

John.

June 26.

John,

Do you really love me? What does it feel like to be in

love, John? Why do you think that you love me? I want to hear more from you. You choose not to tell me about you and Heather. I hope one day you will feel comfortable enough to share with me. I am tired now and will go to sleep and dream of you. I will imagine that I am holding onto your arm, so I can go to sleep.

Simone.

June 28.

Simone,

Please forgive me for what I am about to ask you. You have entered me so deeply that last night I woke up twice with a major startle. I have been full of anxiety ever since; my stomach has been turning. Dream 1. I dreamt that you were taken (at your pleasure) by two men and that the thrill was as you ever wanted it to be. DO YOU EVER THINK OF THIS, STILL? Dream 2. I dreamt you were in a lawyer's office, arguing for custody of your son. Have you ever contested custody?

Tomorrow, I want to greet you with something less harrowing and therefore more cheerful, The Plane. Will we be able to chat on Monday? Even better, could we speak to each other?

John.

June 29.

Sweet darling,

This is good that you are dreaming with such clarity and depth. Did I tell you that I am a lucid dreamer! I used to dream very frequently and while dreaming, I would be conscious of the dream as if I were watching myself in a theatre. Luckily, with the Internet, I found a newsgroup that focuses on this issue in particular. I have discovered that I am not the only one. This is something that some people are, for one reason or another, blessed or cursed, depending on how you see it. I always thought that I should write down my dreams so, over time, I will see a pattern. I rarely have erotic dreams though.

Why do you have such anxiety, my love? Is it the dream or the thought that I may have such fantasies? No, I do not have such fantasies. I do not want to experience such a thing either. When I wrote, I asked if you have thoughts of a threesome or if you experienced such a thing. The thought of being physically with two men, as I said before, is too harsh and not spiritual. I do not know why you would have such a dream. I think there might be an explanation but that really means we are getting very connected if that is the case.

Let me share with you a few things that happened last week. Remember when I told you that I was ending an affair a few weeks ago? Well, I did. Anders went on a vacation and was back last week. He had a car accident and hurt his shoulder and collar bone. He sent me a message about the accident and said that he was feeling really terrible. I saw him this week over lunch. He says that he still loves me. I do not think that he does but I feel that I mean a lot to him; he does care for me. I do care for him but I do not love him. I told him so yesterday as well. When he told me he was injured I really felt concerned for him. That is why I saw him. Maybe that is why you had this dream?

I was wondering very much this week if it is possible to remain friends with him or if I should just be hard enough to cut off all communication. It is a difficult decision to make. I think it is possible to remain friends and care about each other but I fear my own vulnerability. It is really difficult because I like him as a friend but do not want to confuse him either. I was comparing in my mind how I feel towards you and how I feel toward him. There is no doubt in my mind; you are the one I love. You are different, and with you, I feel much higher levels of contact than I have ever experienced in my life with anyone! Anders and I never exchanged what you and I have.

You are so amazing and I really do not know how to say it but you do reach my subconscious with amazing power. You complete me and free me in ways I never thought possible. Our connection is different. I feel like you are a magnet and I am so attracted to you, as if your energy is pulling me to you with such abandonment and strength that I have never experienced before. I told you before that you are extraordinary.

I thought much about the custody question! I have not fought over custody of Zak or Sarah in court. However, the fact that you saw me in a dream doing so is really very curious. Let me share this with you. Two weeks ago, I had these very, very heavy feelings.

I am sure that your mother passed away this year and very recently too. If not that then she must be very sick and maybe on her deathbed and is thinking of you intensely, of that time of separation from you. At one point, I felt my body being used at some level to communicate a message to you. I did focus much on that though. I felt that she was trying to communicate something she never had the chance to do: express something that weighed on her heart for the longest time and somehow, spiritually, is being realised through me. Maybe she is trying to communicate to you directly through dreams.

I am not sure about all of this. It feels very foggy as I do not have the clarity or frame of mind to feel such things. I told you often and I will do so again. Your future is really bright and you will somehow close many gaps in your heart and work. I feel that I will help you in doing so but I do not know how or in what means or why! But that is the way it is, as irrational and unscrupulous as this may sound. We are both in the realm of a paranormal sphere; that I am sure of. I am too tired though and too torn to focus on anything.

I feel like I am drowning and it is only your hand that is pulling me and sustaining me at this point. My head is hurting. I feel like crawling into a dark corner and holding my knees as I sit on the floor and just cry and cry and cry. I may rock myself to sleep as I cry my heart out.

Help me, John. Please! I am too afraid of surrendering to this despair and to losing all control. I must survive. I must! I do not want to think now. I will stop here.

Simone.

June 29.

Darling Simone,

Very quickly, my love, this is unnerving. There were three three questions but I feared to offer the third! My question would have been, "Do you have someone to satisfy your real-time needs?" What is it, my love, that you are uncovering in me and between us? It is so lovely and so real despite our distance. To feel such things is magical (yet at times, rippled with juvenile anxiety – forgive me for that).

John.

July 1.

Simone,

You evaded my question about why no custody battle. I seek not to cause you pain but to simply hear the explanation because my fitful waking caused me to believe that the words you use in rational explanation could be the words my mother might have used! I will not be troubled or offended or hurt or sick. I will simply know. As I have said to you before, I shall always try and get you out of fits of sadness. But the answer to my question remains important. Leave it for now, my love. Tell me when you are ready.

John.

July 2.

John,

Why no custody battle? Well, I will have to answer this question over and over again to Zak in the future! Will he ask why I did not fight to keep him? Will he ask if I loved him? My rationale for not keeping Zak is that I cannot take care of him or his well-being in addition to taking care of Sarah. The burden of taking care of two children and having a full- time job is, well, impossible. I would slowly ebb away as a fighting spirit. I would have to be crazy to even imagine that I could give him the best care. Sarah is too young now and I can manage. Also, my husband is very emotionally attached to Zak. It would crush him to lose Zak. I am even sure that it would cause him severe psychological damage. He is a product of a dysfunctional family – a father who never paid attention to him. He was a father that was never there and never cared to take care of him his whole life. He has very much the same fears that you have for your children.

I weep privately. I feel that it is not fair for me to lose my son even though I believe that it is in his best interests to go with his father. Your mother possibly thought just like me. She possibly regretted it big time! She could have argued to have you back. I do not know what the future holds but I am trying to understand your questions. Did I answer or are you still wondering? Yes, I did not fight! Yes, it was a mutual decision on our parts. Does this make me a horrible mother? Does this make me selfish? I am not sure. It is hard to draw the line for my motives except for my dreadful fear that I will fail in taking care of my beautiful little boy.

Did my custody answer correspond to something that your mother felt? I think so: the dreadful fear of failing to protect my own child; the dreadful fear of not being able to financially provide for two children; the burden of a foreign culture. You, an English child in a foreign country!

I do not know what the future will hold for me or for my children. I have to be strong, I tell myself. I have to endure this failure. Tell me if my answer made you think a bit more about her or not.

John's motive for exploring this relationship had developed on many levels. Yet this aspect seemed to be at the heart of much that was going on in his mind – consciously and subconsciously. After all, he was trying to convey to Simone the impact that might be felt by her son through his own experience at her son's age. In turn, she was, arguably, reflecting what John's mother might have been suffering as she lost her only son. The fact that she was German and his father British, that it was just after World War II and therefore the chances of her winning custody of a British child, through the British military judicial system, in occupied Germany might have had a bearing on everything. He did not, for one moment, suppose that Simone was in an equivalent, unequal situation. What mattered here though was that her anguish might be a reflection of John's mother's own anguish. If so, he was trying not only to understand himself but also to see if he could rid himself of his wider confusions concerning women. Simone seemed the perfect vessel for both.

July 3.

Simone,

There is no failure here, just courage and rationality. The one plausible explanation I was offered many years later was that even if my mother had wanted to keep me, she would have been in an impossible situation to attempt to fight for me. Your decision is rational because you realise that you must survive as well; a strong you is a vibrant you and therefore able to give even more to your son in quality time and support whenever he will need it and whenever he is with you. You are a courageous woman. I applaud you and I applaud that quality. We are two of a kind in many respects.

John.

July 5.

My dear Simone,

I suppose your earlier mystical connections with the possibility of "feeling my mother" sent a shiver through me. I still don't understand why I had those two vivid dreams, both leading to real revelations from you! This is no mere coincidence. I wondered but found myself not yielding to the temptation of such a possibility (her reaching out to me through you in her last days). How could I dare to open myself to such a possibility (my eyes are becoming moist at the thought of letting myself go to such a possibility). Heavens! What a prospect and what a torment for all concerned. This defies all rationality except one. Through the wonders of cyberspace, we have not only found this reincarnation of my boyhood and subsequent yearning for a motherly strength but in my manhood, a return to that terrible start, through your pending loss. No! This is not rational. It isn't even love in the normal or conventional sense, as you described earlier. It is something completely different. It transcends time (as we have seen – my mother; your son and our transposition of these roles; you and me – with all the psychological and therefore sensual permutations that it conjures) and space (our Internet connection from the US to the UK). There must be a profound word for this but I don't know what that might be. Maybe the whole thing comes down to wishful thinking – pure and simple – but that would be an insult.

John.

21.

July 10.

Simone,

'It was a rush and I nearly missed the flight. All the connections were wrong. The taxi driver was useless and the check-in people were screwing around with my ticket – problems of legibility! I was not pleased! While boarding, I lugged my briefcase along the aisle with my notebook computer and a change of clothes inside it; always prepared. I sat down, looked at the stewardess, feigning a gasping sound and suggesting, not too subtly, that I needed some fluid inside me. The tray was on its way anyway but I was trying to show the human side to this rushing passenger that they should take care of this night. It had been a tough trip and a tough day.

I pushed my briefcase, flat, under the seat in front of me. I clasped at the champagne and just lay back. It was an aisle seat – not my favourite. I am usually more conscious of the window-side passenger, making a polite acknowledgement – male or female, old or young. I turned and found myself looking straight into your eyes as you were obviously conscious of me and waiting for the correct moment to make that initial connection. I looked at you again and stumbled my words out. 'Hello! I think you can tell. It's been a bit of a rush!' (Classic English understatement.) Your soft voice intoned a leisurely and relaxing reply. It was hypnotic. I had to steel myself. I shook my head and wondered what on earth was going on. It had been a tough week but not tough to the point of my head starting to reel. I achieved one solid run each day so my body was in peak condition. It was firm and hungry. I was breathing clearly and my blue eyes were penetrating. I only had to wear my glasses to read in the worst of light. We introduced ourselves. We settled and the plane started to move.

I really didn't say much. I shrank into my seat and just munched nuts and drank a little more champagne. I watched the news without taking it in. You were on my mind. I would glance at you and, sometimes, you would turn and just smile. I found myself melting. What on earth was going on? I must be tired or even a little deranged. Whatever it was, it was nice. The meal was served. It was consumed. It was cleared away. Night time settling down was the next order of business.

"Would you excuse me, John?" you asked.

"Of course!" I replied and stood up to help you out. I could have remained seated but that essential need to be courteous was always alive.

I took your hand as I guided you out of the seats. I lingered my clasp and found you squeezing gently. My eyes darted to yours; that smile again. I shivered inside. You returned and I stood up again, helping you in. You were now wearing a pair of loose tracksuit trousers. You wanted to travel with the maximum of comfort and the minimum of restrictions. I was in mine too. The lights were dimmed. TV screens started to be flipped up from their storage places, blankets were unfolded and passengers settled in to sleep.

"Good movies I hope!"

I murmured, half venturing it as an overture to you and half talking to myself. You smiled at me. We settled. Most people were now dozing. The cabin crew had done their interminable rounds and were no more to be seen. I was dreaming my way through the flickering pictures.

Suddenly, your hand moved from under your blanket. You took mine and squeezed with great tenderness. I looked over at you. You were smiling that gorgeous smile of yours. I took courage, raised your hand to my lips, and kissed it gently. You astounded me. You switched the motion round, kissed my hand then gave it a little lick! I shivered again. What was happening here?

The cabin was dark. We could see each other's faces from the light of the TV screens. We settled back down but you kept my hand in your grip. You unbuckled your safety belt and slipped my hand underneath your blanket. I felt the soft warmth of your tummy. I was shaking. You kept my hand firm and guided it under your loose waistband. You were wearing nothing else.

I began to stroke you with my fingers. You knew I was with you now and that you needed no further encouragement. I let my fingers drift lower and, with each inch massaging more of you, I felt the top of your clit and then pushed into your slit. It was inviting. I moved that bit lower and felt the wetness of your pussy. I moved my whole hand in until my palm covered your essence. I caused an air air trap like a suction pad so that you could feel my embrace of your love juices.

I pulled back a little and looked at you. You smiled at me through your flickering eyes. I used my middle finger and pushed gently into your most intimate space. You wanted this. I withdrew, positioned a second finger and pushed them both in. I withdrew again. I prepared for three fingers and slid them all in. You were so wet it was easy. I wiggled them slightly to give you more sensation. You gripped my arm, held me there and started spasms of muffled pleasure. I kept massaging and penetrating. This was not moisture. You were WET. As it poured out I spread it around your inner thighs. You froze, then shivered and then relaxed. I left my hand there to comfort and protect the opening of you.

You responded with no words, just deeds. I helped you up as I stood up too. We moved to the restroom. Even at the front of the plane, they were not big. I opened the door for you and led you in. As I moved in as well, I turned to pull the door and saw a stewardess, looking and smiling with envious acknowledgement and nodding, as if she would bar any attempt to interrupt us. The light was on. We were pressed together. I looked into your eyes then kissed you with force. My tongue compelled your mouth to open. Your tongue responded with equal power. We were breathing with a combined fury. I placed you on the sink and pulled your trousers down. I untied my own and let them fall. You clung to my neck, and I rammed my hands up your blouse to feel the full heat of your breasts. You took a hand away and opened the blouse at the front. I unhooked your bra and revealed the beauty of you. Your nipples became firm and erect. I kissed one then the other. I sucked so sweetly yet so firmly. You moaned. I came up again and kissed you gently and whispered that I wanted you, I needed you, that I was going to have you.

I pulled you forward and found you ready. I pushed my manhood to the initial grip of your desire. You responded with a contraction. I pushed a little further. You gasped. I plunged myself with deep penetration and held that first thrust. Electricity flew right through me. Then it started. I pushed slowly as you gripped my ass hard. You pulled me into you. I started to pump with increased fury and passion. You moaned and kissed me hard.

"Fuck me! Fuck me hard!" Your words excited me. I looked at you for a moment, savouring the passion. We smiled together before launching into serious fucking. From then, words disappeared as I began to sweat. I pushed into you as deep as I could go! It was as if we were rocking the plane from side to side. Pumping, pumping, pumping hard. You gripped me even more fiercely and pulled me into you. Then by some miracle we started erupting together. We were in a spasm as our mutual juices swam into each other. My body arched with pleasure. You clung deeper and harder. Ah! Joy!

We rested, totally spent. I put you on to the sink again to let you sit and rest a moment. You cradled your head on my shoulder and whimpered words of adoration. I kissed your ear.

"Are you okay?" I asked with genuine concern.

"I'm wonderful," you replied, "and so are you!" I could see that you were settled now but I needed one more thing. I needed to heal the friction in your pussy and on your clit. I knelt down. I looked inside the pink mass of pleasure and wetness. My tongue caressed your clit. It was warm. I moved to your pussy and licked you clean. My mouth swam with our mutual joy. I held it and came up to your lips. You opened in full expectation. I kissed you and let it flow from over my tongue and onto yours. You swallowed and kissed me long and deeply. We were at peace.

We returned to our seats, wrapped each other in our blankets, took each other's hand and fell asleep in rapturous slumber.'

John.

22.

Dearest sweet John,

I went back to sleep after I read your messages this morning. Later, I finished my coffee and opened them again. What a true yet exquisite description of our (apparently sometimes haunting) relationship.

What a wonderful gift you sent me today as well. I loved every line and every gesture. It was truly, truly perfect to a point where I was really feeling wet. The pleasure of your touch and the thought of your hand caressing me is absolutely fantastic. I read it twice and felt much happiness flow over my body.

You write so beautifully, John. It is so sweet and so tasteful. John, I really feel connected to you in a way that is so wonderful and beyond the bounds of reality. I love you so much. I look forward to hearing your voice again on Monday. I would love to hear you moan with pleasure as you call my name. I cannot tell you how electrically satisfying this voice of yours is. You are so special and so lovely.

This morning I had such an amazing experience. It was very, very amazing, as if I was outside my body and my fingers were typing away at the command of your mother. Maybe I imagined it. Maybe it is my subconscious; I do not not know. I find it a leap of imagination to say maybe at some point this was a trans-channelling experience that I had. It is possible but I fear the recognition of such a thing. My comfort is that it is you in which I am confiding. I am sure you will understand.

Are you happier than you were before we met? I sure am. I am actually much happier. I feel that my journey ahead is not as frightening. I used to have these sickening anxiety attacks where I would totally feel helpless. I can only wonder what is in store for us when we meet.

Simone.

July 12.
Simone,

It's lunchtime this Sunday and the weather is beautiful. I walked into the kitchen and said to Heather, "Wouldn't it be good if—(dreaming about a remote but possible job option for the future)." She just turned and told me not to upset myself with those dreams and proceeded with the practical things of this world. I don't blame her for she has had a tough time but it just made me realise that at one level at least, you are so much more in tune with my dream-world reality. I miss the contact with you, the immediacy of you. I went into my study and sat for a moment, looking at the blank computer screen, wondering where you were at this moment. She came in and asked what I was doing. I said nothing and returned to our domestic reality. Despite the reality of homecomings and the delight of the children, my relationship with Heather, beyond the practicalities of living together, is zero. We still sleep in the same bed but, as I said before, I avoid going up at the same time as her – using lame excuses. It could be depression. I still love her (maybe like a sister but I am certainly not 'in love' with her now. From her point of view, it was such a pity because she had done nothing, absolutely nothing, to cause this emotional demise.

John.

Now, John was being altered. He felt adventurous. He wanted more. He had tapped into things that needed to be explored. From an outsider's perspective, it was he who was selfish as well as being dishonest. From his perspective, he was trying to retain enthusiasm for life, to help carry him through the challenges of his home. That centred on Heather and his loss of an essential, passionate love for her.

July 14.
Good morning!
This is surely a lovely day. I will have breakfast, take some tea with my mother, sit with her out on the deck, and enjoy Sarah. Our neighbours have a little dog. Our decks are parallel so he sticks his head and barks at Sarah. She finds that quite funny. I will go to the gym afterwards. It is ten days now! I feel so rusty and the reason why I did not go for so long is that I was sick and then I had my period.

I must go now. My mother is calling me for breakfast. I

miss you so much and you are so unbelievably always, always with me.

Simone.

July 15.

Simone,

I shall be awake in five hours and traveling in six! Just looking at your pictures again and replaying your lovely voice in my head and looking at the gentle curves of your breasts and imagining them and you in full and naked repose, waiting to be taken by the gentle being that I am sometimes, longing to kiss the warmth of your lips, before exploring more intimate areas of your body and your soul.

I really hope we will have a chance to speak tomorrow night; I shall send you a message from the hotel when ready!

I still marvel at what has happened to us; never in my wildest dreams was such beauty a possibility. I thought this would lead to a little sympathy and understanding at best.

Look at us now! You're a marvel. I adore you!

John.

July 16.

Darling!

In five hours or so I will hear your voice! I only wonder what conversation we will have. I want to tell you how much I missed hearing your tender laughs and how much I love you. Let me know what your number is.

Simone.

July 16.

Simone,

Now you know, you gorgeous woman! Thank you for such a sublime and beautifully messy covering of my tummy. One day, my darling! One day! I shall go to sleep stroking your hair and telling you not to worry, my little girl. My arm is around you, and I love you so.

You sweet beautiful girl. Let me stroke your hair again and touch the grace of your back and your shoulders. Let me love and protect you, my darling!

John.

July 16.
John,
My love, my darling, my angel! I cannot explain how I feel but it is glorious! I have never been so happy. I totally trust you and totally surrender myself to you. You wonderful, wonderful angel!

July 16.
John,
How do you know how to make me feel so good? How do you know to make me feel so loved? I was shuddering with so many mixed feelings all day today. I love you.

July 16.
Simone,
Tell me, my love. What are these mixed feelings you have? I adore you!

July 16.

Darling!

You ask me what these mixed feelings are. Joy and content content is really what I feel. I also fear losing this wonderful connection with you. You touch my heart in ways I never thought possible. It is not only love that I feel but inner spiritual completeness. Beyond that, I worry about my ability to support myself and my little girl and cover all the bills that I will be taking care of very soon. I worry about not being able to travel to see my son (again, a financial concern). I worry about not being able to bring my mother and father here or not being able to travel to Spain (another financial concern). I am not a planner when it comes to money and have terrible habits of spending without thinking. I have started to monitor myself and have become more aware. The cost of living in the US is really high. I worry about Sarah's well-being. It is critical for me to focus on my career and be the best I can so I can better provide for Sarah and Zak. These are my pressing practical concerns at this point really. I am a lousy financial planner. I know that if I did have a good plan, I might be able to cover all that I need and meet all my goals.

Also, I will lose most of my furniture and decorative items soon and that is really bothering me but it is part of the separation deal. I have to re-finance next year to assume the mortgage once I divorce. I am not sure what the interest rates will be and how much money I need to bring down the payment of my house.

I worry about my emotional well-being. You are so wonderful and are such a protective spirit. I need to be strong and not to cave in to impulse. I worry about my physical needs and if that will make me do things that I will regret! I do not see myself re-marrying ever or having a boyfriend or any committed relationship (as in a couple-like arrangement). I just cannot do that. I do not want to do that. I have you now and that is great.

Anders and I are having hard time. The reason is really that I do not feel that he understands me emotionally or my needs. No one does except you. Yes, I could say to myself he is such a nice person and very safe to satisfy my physical needs but that is bothering me terribly. I have never thought I had to separate these two aspects of my being. I told you before that these two aspects are intertwined and connected – and spiritually, it makes me feel very empty. However, I am also human and do recognize my vulnerability so that scares me.

These are my practical concerns. How will you help me sort these things out? I love you. I want to be your little girl you know. I want you to protect me and give me guidance about decisions I have to make. Once upon a time, a long time ago I was my daddy's little girl. Everything I achieved was for his pride and I loved the attention and the care and the pride he had for me. It made me feel safe. It made me feel secure and confident. Today I feel very disconnected from such emotion as I rarely get a chance to communicate with him. I am a grown woman now and both distance and marriage severed this emotional support.

This morning, while I was taking a shower, I felt so

free and so liberated. It was such an exhilarating experience for me to recognise that my marriage is coming to an end. It is such a good thing that I found enough courage to do this. It is a three year decision in the making and it was a rough, rough ride so…

I do not know what the future holds for me.

Simone.

July 18.

My dearest, sweetest, most loveable Simone,

I have your letter in hard copy in front of me. Let's put the financial thing in perspective. I remember you were despondent once before. I pointed out certain things to you that were totally in your favour. You may not be so sure at present but when you read about the reality of my situation, you will come to understand this! First, you *have* a job and, I infer, a good one. There are prospects for it to get better and for you to benefit from that financially, right? I assume this is all true and that you are earning a reasonable salary now, yes? Again, I assume yes! So you operate from relative strength or financial autonomy (what would it be like if you had no job?).

Don't lose heart, my love. Inner strength is important, though!

Harness yours!

Sometimes *I* despair but I keep it to myself (until now; this is the first time I have put down my thoughts on my 'here and now', though I have been thinking of it for a while).

If I can offer you anything it will be the will to fight and succeed. I have just come to the point of fighting forces beyond even my strength.

In May this year, I put out my last cry for help. You have been with me ever since. Please stay with me, my love, and let me stay with you (my eyes water just a little and I sigh, simply longing to give you a protective squeeze and for you to embrace me closely).

To my dearest Simone, stay with me forever!
John.

July 19.
John,

I am with you. I am with you now and tomorrow and forever. The foggy one was the "physical needs". Yes, I like Anders and he is a very nice person. He is married, so I do not have to worry about his desire to have a committed relationship. I am very passionate but I am very conservative. I am not a wild person. I do not go to bars and I do not lightly consider any physical encounter. My fear is that today I am happy and free and so glad to have this marriage finish. Yes, I do believe that there should be an emotional extension to the physical one and that's where the trouble begins.

If I do not care, then there is no issue, right? I do like Anders but I do not think that I love him. I am not sure about him and what he feels but I know that he deeply cares about me.

I guess I will just let these things take their course and not worry too much about it. I got to go now. I hope to chat today at three o'clock, my time.

Simone.

John simply did not understand this sentence: 'If I do not care, then there is no issue right?' What was she suggesting? That in her need for the physical, if she did not care too much emotionally, it was perfectly justifiable to have the physical experience. If so, then she was thinking like the average selfish man. There was no reason for her not to think that way but it belied her need for the strong emotional bond. Was this drifting back to notions of experimentation – two women, or even two men. Would such experimentation involve him or not? In any case, what on earth was he getting flustered about. This was, after all, a cyber-relationship. It had all the hallmarks of easy entry and exit. The emotional spillovers were genuine and, at times, really heartfelt. Yet he felt uneasy with these thoughts. What right had he to feel any kind of possessiveness, let alone exclusiveness? None! So, what did he do? He reverted to his own selfishness in order to draw attention away from others and back to him. He sent her another strong scenario!

23.

July 24.

Simone,

'I was impatient and dispensed with the niceties of foreplay. I didn't need to fuck you. I needed to consume you. Your clothes were seized and removed without subtlety. Your nakedness revealed a vulnerable beauty. On this occasion, it was to be conquered. I was hungry. I needed the potential rawness of your passion. Mine was already vibrant. You wondered what to do. You started tearing at my clothes. I helped you. Within seconds I was naked too, erect and ready to plunge myself into you. I threw you onto the bed and turned you onto your front.

I leapt on you and pressed down, showing you that this time you were completely in my power. I wanted to envelope you in my total desire. You tried to move but I kept you pinned down with my force. I stretched your arms in front of you and pushed my hands along your arms until my hands met yours. I held them and squeezed to show momentary mercy for you. As we stretched together, you could feel the power of my erection flirting with your ass slit.

I slammed myself down, aiming at nothing in particular. You were startled and let out a quiet scream. I leapt up and and turned myself around. My face was now on your ass. I pushed your legs apart, keeping your shoulders pinned down with my legs. I tickled the entrance to your asshole with my tongue. I pushed to tease you. You tried to close yourself but I kept your legs apart with my arms. 'Push your ass up,' I said. You did, with fear. The greater access to your most intimate part let my tongue slip into that delicate place. As soon as you felt it, you pushed higher to let me get even deeper into you. My tongue lunged into your secret folds. You were already so wet. My impatience was uncontrollable.

I spun round again and before I had even taken hold of you properly, my vast erection was plunging itself deep inside you. Your head rested on your forearms and rocked forward and back to the rhythm of my deep and penetrating fucking of you. I needed to consume this beautiful woman whose ass was waiting for me! I was upright from my knees, holding your ass cheeks tight to maintain a firm grip of my woman as I fucked and fucked and fucked again. I started to moan, knowing that my time was coming. I heard you start to erupt as well.

I kept pushing as hard and as deep as I possibly could. "Fucking whore, my beautiful fucking whore!"

The surge started to come and as it flowed through me and into you, I heard and felt your spasm of orgasmic pleasure shoot forth. We came together like teenage lovers. We rested a second to reflect on the satisfaction of its mutual power then collapsed in a heap. I wrapped my arms around you and we

fell asleep.'
John.

July 25.
John!
Absolutely lovely!

July 27.
My dearest Simone,
To love you is to feel your physical (and emotional) needs. That should be satisfied by me but they obviously can't be! The emotional can but not the physical. You are in a catch22! You need physical pleasure (but to deny emotion is to deny you – you turn yourself into something else). Yet, to seek emotional and physical fulfilment means that you might fall in love again. That is something you simply cannot avoid (if Cupid strikes)! I just ask you to be careful for your emotional sake and treat your physical needs tenderly (as I would so love to do). I would love to come and protect you forever!
John.

July 28.
Simone,
I do hope we can talk tonight before I leave, my love. I'm on the rooftop terrace on the seventeenth floor of the hotel, looking out. The city is concentrated and almost poetic with its dulcet tones of gentle noise and the sporadic call to prayers.

I finished my work at five p.m. today, went to the general manager's office to bid my farewell but found him absent. Instead, his two delectable assistants were there. They said "farewell" as if they meant it – regretting I was leaving as early, as I was. I was touched by the manner of their concern and their wish that I would return. I took a sunbed and for the first time this trip, just lay for half an hour, letting the sun kiss my body. Earlier today, colleagues said it was hot at 38°C. It was a very dry heat and therefore very comfortable for me.

I lay and thought how I was descending into despondency; leaving this place, the care and the thought that, through work, I am a reasonably important person. I am returning to a grey reality. I thought about leaving the freedom to write messages almost at will (instead of having to snatch time at home). I thought of you and wondered what you were doing at this moment and why I couldn't just be there with you. I thought of thoughts no strong man contemplates – just the soft gentle touch of love, placing her hand upon my shoulder, kissing my cheek and telling me that I was really loved and not to worry because everything will be all right...

John.

July 31.

Darling,

I look outside my office window and I see a pond; a small little pond where geese and ducks come to drink as they thirst for water in this wretched heat. It is very humid and this weather on a Friday is leaving everyone with a desire to do nothing but daydream about the golden moment when this day will come to an end. I dream of you. I think of you and I feel so much love for you pulsating and reverberating over every cell in my body.

How could this be? you ask me. Just let it be because of my love. You asked me about your voice and how it feels. It rings in my heart not in my ears. You sweet angel. How much I want to shield you from your own vulnerability. You are so much in need of my love. I can see that. I can feel it. I want to hold you forever and stroke your hair as I whisper in your ear stories of love and passion.

My brave, tired warrior. You are in so much pain but that is okay, my love. You just close your eyes and come to my arms and lay there and go to sleep. I watch over you as you sleep. I ward off the forces of evil and keep you safe and protected. You will need to worry no longer as you breathe deep and dream away times of happiness and content.

Today you were very special on the phone. I cannot imagine not hearing from you for two weeks but I will wait and re-read what you sent me.

Simone.

John's pain was the realization that his marriage was a shadow of what it should be and that his cyber-relationship was just that. If that relationship did not exist, his spirits would have been much lower. If his e-love was warding off depression, then that was a good thing, was it not? Anyway, he consoled himself with the cyber-reality as well as the latest dimension – sometimes, electrifying phone sex. As a side-issue: phone sex is commonplace now, especially with the availability of Skype video calls, for example. The first time John was aware of it was in the original British film Get Carter; *there's a phone sex sequence as Carter (played by Michael Caine) calls from his dingy Newcastle accommodation to his girlfriend (played by Britt Ekland) in London. The novelty is that the film was made in 1971, well before mobile phones, let alone the wondrous medium known as the internet – a medium John was harnessing with some success.*

July 31.

Darling,

I can still hear the sound of you whacking your precious cock. What a lovely sound and how much I yearned to take it between my hands and glide it right inside me as I rode you astride. The fullness of you is incredible…

'As my juices overflow your hard erection, I command you to lay face down. I push you on the bed and ask you to raise your ass. You obey. I take your wet cock between my hands as I spread your legs farther. Your balls are right there in front of me to massage and to caress.

"Don't move!" I say, and I spank you really hard on your left cheek.

"Keep your ass up. Do not move and do not look either!"

You are excited. I can see this in your erection. I keep on gently massaging your balls and hard cock. I kneel down as my breasts brush your ass. You feel my hair. I kiss your left cheek where I spanked you and it is burning red. I start licking you there and kissing and licking more. I move to the other cheek as I keep on massaging your erection. I kiss and lick your other cheek.

As I hold both cheeks apart, I can see the round rim of your ass beckoning me. I fill my hand with my mouth's fluid and glide it right there down the crack of your ass to your rim. You moan and shiver with desire. I spank you hard again on the other cheek.

"I told you do not move." You are totally under my mercy now. Wanting me to fuck you right there. You surrender your body to me. I own you now. You are my slave and I will do whatever I please with you.

I use my tongue on your balls and lick them so gently. My tongue traces the gentle caresses of your balls down your cock, all from the back as your ass is up in the air open for me to take you.

"Do you want me to take you?"

You say, "yes! Please, please take me. YES!"

I know exactly what you want. I will give it to you and you will love it. My tongue goes a little higher to the area between your rim and balls and circles around and around as you writhe under my grip. I go a little further and tease your asshole with my tongue. You are so desperate now for me to fuck you.

I kiss you right there at the entrance of your rim and deposit my fluid as my finger finds its way into you. I push my finger gently and you cry. I hold your cheeks tight with one hand as I push my finger deeper. You are tense and you tighten up, so I push harder. You relax and I position myself to fuck you with force and fury. I push another finger and you cry again. I fuck you very, very hard and you feel the pressure of my fingers inside swelling and exploding spasms of orgasm that is not coming yet. My other hand is still massaging your lovely huge cock. I decide that it is enough and pull my fingers out. I command you to lie on your back. You do. I turn around and ride your face as I slide my wet pussy to your eager tongue. You take me and I take your cock all the way into my mouth as I feel yours sliding inside me, eating my dripping juices. We both moan. My head is exploding with desire and you too writhe and writhe with pleasure. We both build up and climax together and explode. Your fluid shoots into my mouth. Your fluid overflows into my mouth and I drink you. I drink every drop as my tongue licks your erection. I scream with pleasure as you wipe me clean with your precious tongue. You insert a finger into me to maximise my pleasure and I ride you frantically with force and power. I climax with shuddering orgasm. I pull out and drop on the bed groaning with erotic pleasure. You lay on top of me, pin me down and cover me up with your lovely warm body and enclose me between your arms. You whisper in my ears, "I love you".'

Simone.

August 4.

Darling!

I re-read my last naughty e-mail to you. I just cannot believe I wrote that stuff! I am actually now smiling and my eyes are sparkling with mischief. How on earth did I do this? What propels me to do such a thing, I do not know. I

know one thing. You are my precious and beautiful darling.
    Simone.

*It had come to a point where John had encouraged or even tempted
Simone to tap into her dark side, if indeed it was the dark side.
It was certainly an explicit side. There was no cruelty. There was a
little role-playing but which adventurous couples do not? What was
really interesting was that Simone had even written this scene
without being prompted to do so. Was she ripe for more, he
wondered. Would he 'push the envelope'? Would he see how far he
could go within himself and thereby thrill Simone into even more
revelations? It had certainly distracted her from her soul-searching
about Anders!*

*The equally fascinating thing was that he had no
compunction about this journey in relation to his marriage.
It was a parallel universe he was inhabiting and a very
fulfilling one for its lack of realism. Could the word schizophrenia
be apposite at this point? He really didn't know, and frankly
he could not care less what words others might use to categorise
what was happening here. He just knew that, without this
experience, his morale, such as it was, might have collapsed by
now.*

24.

August 5. Simone,

Our telephone call was absolutely lovely! I have replayed it in my mind to the point of heavenly pleasure. You are so beautiful. Your voice is like that of an angel. It thrills me in my secret parts... You are perfection!

Since meeting you online, I have been virtually transformed as a human being. I may still be in an awful state but you have given me inner strength.

John.

The conversation was good for two reasons. First, they had another round of explosive phone sex. They then started to talk seriously about the possibility of John visiting New York.

Simone.

Can we say that I arrive on Thursday, 26th October? It seems like becoming an increasing possibility! Would you come out to JFK in your Corolla (great cars by the way)? If you were driving, how would you cope with my hand on your arm, on your knee or even on your thigh? You are so lovely! Again, our last phone conversation was delicious! I replay it in my mind. I express things to you that have never come out of my mouth, let alone my heart, before. I need and want you so badly, at times even desperately, but at this moment just nice and calmly.

Be my love forever as I am yours to cherish and adore. See! If I was with you, I would be saying these things to you! Do your brown eyes sparkle?

John.

August 8.

My precious and special John,

Yes, I will come to JFK and pick you up. Hmm; what a delicious possibility. What wonder and excitement and knee-deep butterflies will I have while waiting. Yes, October 26th would be great. How will I drive back home – that is something I do not know; somehow we will manage. I can see you now riding next to me "for a change!" Though, I prefer it when you ride on top of me. I will look at you and steal a few glances and take deep breaths as my heart pounds away.

John, there are only twenty days left till the dreadful separation of August 29th – that black horrible, horrible day. What am I to? My son comes to me now and hugs me and tells me that he loves me, and I shudder with tears. Sarah will be with my mother for the first two months and I am grateful to her as I know that I will not be in an emotional state to focus on Sarah's precious little needs. I am not afraid but I know that the pain is going to be something so horrible.

I just had a tiny 'chat' with you! You are so wonderful, my beautiful John. Yes, I will calm down. My husband is telling me how hurt he is over losing me. He tells me that he still loves me. He quizzes me about whether I have found a lover. He remonstrates over how I destroyed our family.

I wonder with shock. Is it me who destroyed the family? I succumb to my guilt and fear for such a horrible thought.

Three years ago I decided to pull things through for the family. I thought I was doing the right thing. Here I am today and I just cannot do this again. I just cannot stay for the sake of the family or the children. I just cannot live with him. I do love him but not as a lover. He is the father of my children. For that, he will always have a special place in my heart. Yet I cannot bear to be lured back into this marriage for duty and 'the honourable thing to do'. In the morning he said, "I cannot wait to leave for California and not see your face!" In the evening he is lamenting my evil destruction of the family. I must tell you one day how all this mess happened but not now. I am tired and will try to get more rest now.

Please stay with me and help me be strong. I cannot see things clearly and my mind is shrouded with all kinds of complexities. Help me. I will draw on you for my strength.

Simone.

August 10.
My lovely Simone,
One thing you must realise is that the writing I offer you is that which you have uncovered in me, which you have

generated from me and that which you have inspired from me! Without you, these qualities and these thoughts would have lain dormant, probably forever. What a grim thought!

Let me get this Thursday business absolutely clear. Are you saying that you could be off on Thursday and Friday, or just Thursday afternoon but all of Friday. If you were off on Thursday as well, I would try and arrive late Wed so that we have that night of bliss as well! Anyway, let me know. Looking at flights, by way of example, KLM seems to get in at two thirty p.m. so, what is your preference, for me to arrive on a Wednesday or Thursday. If this actually happens, I would love to take your hand at the airport, go to a coffee shop and just sit and talk a little so that we make that final physical connection after all the other awe inspiring links we have realised so far. Then we could travel in the car and I would sit a little more calmly (and you would drive a little more sedately), and we would indeed ride side-by-side. (I would be on top later, my love – how delicious you are!) It is so thrilling and so tantalizing and so possible – unless something awful was to intervene but I hope not, I truly hope not.

You have inspired me to survive and therefore, I owe this journey to you, as well as to me and to us!

I put the children to bed tonight. Moira became very emotional – "I don't want you to die, Daddy!" I told her that I didn't want to either and that she wasn't to worry! As I mentioned before, I think, she is a very passionate little thing and will break hearts when she's older or find herself in pain at times. Then she settles down with a smile and starts asking questions like, "why do people have eyebrows, Daddy?" Heather and I are fine, in a superficial way.

Andrew is running around with Heather in the sitting room; she is trying to settle him before I take him to bed. Graham is still out playing; it's nine twenty p.m. He should have been home at nine! I'm on the verge of driving off to try and find him. This happened once before, about a year ago. He was fine, just playing and not thinking about the time!

I drove off and found Graham with his friends, meandering home. He came running over. "You're meant to be home at nine!" I said sternly. "Dad, Dad, we were comparing muscles!" as I suppose boys of his age would do. How could I resist such an explanation? He's home now! I can hear Heather talking to him, conveying notions of concern and the need for responsibility from him.

'What am I to do . . . the pain will be something so horrible.' My love, on this you are going to have to brace yourself and think about the underlying reasons why this has come about and realise that you had no other choice if you were to survive as a vibrant person. As you say to me, we can't sacrifice our whole family for one child, no matter how cruel that seems, so you cannot sacrifice yourself; to do so would be to miss the point entirely. Your first loyalty is to yourself – your well-being, your strength and to retain that ability to be strong for yourself and others. Your second is to your youngest child – the mother-baby thing. Then come any other children.

Yes, pain there will be and torrents of tears, but the pain will ease and the freedom you will experience will gradually replace the awfulness of the particular moment. Whatever the reasons, there should be no blame when a marriage breaks up, simply the intention to do it with the least fuss possible and the smoothest of transitions – no acrimony, if that is possible, but certainly no blame. Never consider yourself as being worthy of 'being blamed'. It takes two to make a marriage and two to end it. His desire to leave in the morning and then to lament the end (in the evening) is a sign of weakness. Having agreed to enter the process of divorce to end it, that is it.

I sense his potential jealousy of your freedom and how you will use it. He should have thought of that a long time ago. On this matter, you are courageous, and I am with you. The marriage has ended. Your freedom beckons. Pain remains to be experienced but that will pass! You owe yourself some happiness. Seize it with both hands.

John.

August 11.

John,

Yes, Wednesday is best in the evening. Arrive then if you can. I will take both Thursday and Friday off. Then we will have Saturday and Sunday and however long you would like to stay while I am at work.

Your e-mail is very soothing. You give me strength, you give me life and for that I am ever so eternally grateful. Yes, I would like to meet you in the airport and sit for a while chatting and drinking coffee – my favourite Starbucks coffee. I miss you and will write later, my precious beautiful angel.

Love, Simone.

25.

August 11.

My sweet darling John,

Your words are healing and rejuvenating my spirit. You are doing so much and more. I love you with all my heart. I pinch myself for this bliss of having you in my life.

Yes, then Wednesday it is and I pray that all the good spirits will be with us. I long for that moment, John, and dream much of that first moment of seeing you. It will be magical and beautiful. I keep on playing your voice in my mind over and over and it is pure as spring water and as precious as the morning dew. It quenches my thirst for you and it calms me down. I hear joy and so much strength in your voice. I hear naughtiness (which is more than good; it is lovely) and I hear mischief. You must have been a mischievous child, John.

Darling, I bought a rug today. I know it was very stupid decision but I fell in love with it. It is so, so pretty and I was just like a child in a candy store. I could not resist the beauty and the magic that it radiated to my heart. I do love rugs so much and this one was a wonderful, wonderful treat to get. It is a Tabriz rug from Iran. It will be shipped to me in five days. The colours are dark royal red and blue, with much, much ornate geometrical designs. Oh, John, if you could only see this rug (and you will!). I am so, so excited! The seller will send me a picture, so I will shoot you a copy. I plan to place it down in the living room where my TV is located. Tomorrow my equipment arrives from Sears. Yesterday, I spent much of the evening setting up the TV stand. I know that all these expenses are not wise and I know that in a way it is reckless. At some level I recognise this but for now, my love, I am happy.

I was so much in love with my father (pure parental love). I was so much in love with him to a point where I could not stand him playing or paying attention to my other siblings. I was *his* world, *his* girl, *his* pride and joy. I would comb his hair and I would hug him, and, so many times, listen to his heartbeat. I remember when I was around eleven to fifteen, I used to have anxiety attacks over fear of losing him to death. I would cry if he was late from work and I would wait for him. He loved me so much and encouraged me to the fullest. Without him I would have never married my husband. I worship him, and to this day he is my joy and the apple of my eye. I miss him so much and miss him encouraging me and telling me that nothing is more important than confidence. He used to tell me lines of poetry about honour and courage and friendship. A very, very gentle, lovely man he is. As I grew up and after I was eighteen, our relationship changed a little. There is a distance that formed in terms of me being a grown woman and all that crap! I wish I were a little girl still basking in his love! I miss him.

John, you are a great father! The way you describe your children and how you take care of them is so, so lovely. Please do not despair. I know it is so hard for me to say that and for you to believe it but you will find happiness in your work.

I have to tell you that I love the way you talk. Honestly! I think it is so wonderful how you utter the words with so much intonation and focus. I love the way you talk. It is so, so special to me and it is really sexy! Do not laugh but it is! I swear. OK, my eyes are twinkling now.

In four days you leave for your vacation. I will not be sad my love. Yes, you do have a brilliant way of expressing erotica in writing! You should write more as you excel in this expression.

I am getting tired now, my love, so I will go to sleep and dream of you. Today I imagined us dancing together, embracing, and you leading me, showing me how to dance. I felt really happy.

Today I also thought that you are so, so smart and I am so lucky to have met you. Did I tell you that I find intelligence very erotic! OK! I got to go now, my love.

Hugs and kisses.
Simone.

August 14.
My love,

A wide-ranging message from my angel. I play in my mind the thoughts that will race through me as I come off the plane and walk through the passport and customs checks; I will have no case to claim. I'll travel light, with a suite carrier. That first touch! That first kiss! That first lingering embrace and to feel the imprint of your body against my chest, and remember, I find it difficult to walk with an erection!

'You must have been a mischievous child, John!' Not really. I was too nervous and introverted. But I do remember in my grandmother's hotel, trying to flirt with the waitresses (I was about seven) and asking them to lie on top of me! Some did!

It is very interesting to hear about your love for your father (that is Moira absolutely!). You have become a very erotic and passionate woman and I suspect she will too. As I said before, I just want her to be prepared for such things, physically and emotionally, so that when the time comes, she experiences such pleasures as a journey of exploration and fulfilment.

You are very sweet about my speaking style. One day you shall hear it in the flesh as I whisper words of deep love and erotic reality (no fantasy; the real thing) into one ear then the other...

You have lifted me from nowhere and given me spirit and adventure in my mind and, indeed, all over my body. Our last telephone conversation was so delicious. When we make love, I shall talk to you. Do you like the idea of me speaking to you and using rough words at rough moments, naughty words at naughty moments, passionate words at passionate moments and loving words at loving moments? At some point, will you let your juices come over my face and my mouth? Will you let me kiss your pussy with my full mouth and my tongue, deep in penetration. Will you scream (a little) with ecstasy and tell me you love me so?

John.

August 15

My darling, good morning!

I just read your e-mail first thing in the morning. I love you so much. No matter how much I repeat it, I just cannot get enough of you, my precious John. I think of that moment of seeing you for the first time. I remember hearing your voice for the first time and how my heart was beating so hard I thought it would burst! I think of myself sitting waiting for you. I will take a book to make the time pass by fast. I will be there half an hour or an hour earlier than your expected arrival time just in case you come earlier. I cannot miss that sweet moment of seeing you coming out of the gate or even watching you come off the plane! I know that I will recognise you immediately.

Your erotic writing is fantastic! It is very, very sensual and lovely.

I've got to run now. You are my life, my happiness and my strength.

Simone.

August 15.

Simone,

'Find yourself a dress that is no longer required; one that can be discarded. Wear it. Imagine yourself with hands tied, above your head, attached to the top of a closed door. The door is closed so that you cannot simply pull away. You are there. I come in and look at you.

"Well, my exquisite woman, my fucking whore, I am going going to fuck you hard!" You look with wonder and thrill simultaneously. I move closer; no subtlety this time. I take hold of the top of your dress, at the neck. I pull, to tear. I rip. I look at you. I rip a little more. You moan and scream a little but quietly. Your breasts become more visible. I rip down to your waist. You have a bra on. I remove it with force. Your breasts are suspended in ripe anticipation. I take a nipple in my mouth. I suck, then rest it between my teeth. I squeeze, then bite until you cry "911." I let go. The other gets the same. I stand back.

"You fucking whore, get those pants off."

Before you have worked out how to do that with your hands tied, I have lunged at you and torn them off too, as the dress is completely ripped apart and discarded on the floor. You are naked except for your shoes. I let you keep them on – a sort of modest perversion! My shirt is opened two buttons down. My chinos are closed but bulging. My cock is hot. 'You're going to get it right now, fucking whore!' I unzip my trousers, pull out the majestic beast and flaunt it at you, showing you the pink glow of its head and the glistening of the 'pre-cum' already very evident. I thrust your legs apart. I lick my fingers and insert them in you. You are ready (ready or not, but you are!). I move in for the kill! Position, entry point, final manoeuvre, then an explosive thrust. You gasp! I start pumping like an animal. You call out. I reply, "Shut up, fucker, and just be fucked like the whore you are!" You muffle desired sounds. I thrust like the pistons of an engine. Hard and deep I go. My arms are stretched up, leaning on the door, the inner arms caressing your ears. I fuck so hard and take your mouth with mine. I thrust my tongue deep inside. My mouth is very wet. I let wetness flow into yours and let you pour your anxiety into me. Harder and harder and harder I fuck you. You start moaning. Your cum has started. I feel the surges beginning from my balls. We now move together and finally explode in orgasmic paradise. "You fucking whore, you fucking beautiful whore. You are my whore! Only for me!" You weaken. Your legs are trembling. I let your arms down and untie you slowly. I rip off the rest my clothes. I take you to bed. I hold you from your back. I caress you. Soon you fall asleep.'

John.

August 15.

My violent angel,

You make my whole body shudder with excitement! My mind and heart are dizzy with rapture. How can you do this? How do you know the deepest of my needs. Yes, I need all your words in roughness, in passion, in love and above all I need you. I need your essence. I need to consume you, to absorb every cell and breath of you – you, my precious and beautiful John. I do need to hear you speaking to me and commanding me. I want to be filled with your voice and to be fully under your control.

Simone.

August 16.

My sweetest love,

I am trying to compose something to illustrate your desire for being conquered by me. I have stopped part way because I fear what I am doing – that it is uncovering something in me I never knew I had. Let me just outline the scene.

'You are sullen and show no interest. I have tried to talk with you but nothing. I am primed and ready. You resist gentle overtures one more time. I switch to the other option and start my pleasure by taking you. Do I pursue such a description for you, my beauty?'

You know in the end that I will love and cherish you! It just may be a tempestuous path to get there this time!

John.

August 17.

My sweetest John,

I am at this point just as you are! I am worried by these manifestations and what we are uncovering in each other. I want to slow down a bit, not for anything in particular, just because I love you and I am at this point afraid of my inner self. I do not want to unleash energies in you and in myself that we would both regret. Maybe we are better to discuss such thing in person. What do you think?

I just came from the gym today. I rode a cardiovascular bike for half an hour and burned two hundred and fifty calories. Then I took the weightlifting for an hour and did all my sit ups and added two new machines. I feel great and my face is very healthy.

I love you so much, John. I cherish you and adore you. We are both treading a dangerous path now I think. It feels like we are both two trains running into each other full speed by force of attraction. We need to slow down, my love. I need to slow down. I want to show you more love on the emotional side. I want to tell you sweet things and cuddle you and hug you, my sweetest darling.

Simone.

This, of course, was not what he wanted to read at all! He was genuinely cautious so as not to presume – to assume too much. What he really wanted was her encouragement, her need for more and more of the darker side. His caution was almost as a child seeking reassurance from a parent – a mother – so that after her smile, he could continue with his naughty little game. In this case, it was neither 'naughty' nor 'little'. It was dark and fundamental; to be 'fundamental' is anything but 'little'.

August 18.

My dearest Simone,

This is so interesting. Once you introduced me to The General, I wrote, then you strengthened it, feeling I was holding back, which I was, for the reasons you supposed. Mutual energy is to be applauded but being taken in certain ways? Yes, I fear that! I want to dominate you at times and, yes, I want to consume you but at my most basic. I want to achieve these two luxuries with love and deep adoration, with a sensual pleasure that will bond us for eternity, whatever else happens to us in the real (and painful) world. I just need to consume you with love and deep, thrusting penetration. I want to consume you in all ways and to be consumed by you. I want you to envelope me with your love for all time.

John.

August 18.

My John,

I do not have much time to tell you – have a great time and enjoy your vacation. I barely had time to get this message in! I love you and miss you and will be thinking of you.

Simone.

By now John was bursting. He had read her caution with dismay. She was correct, of course, but the little boy inside him was wanting to 'play some more' with his new metaphorical toy – domination (at her original request!) – and, therefore, to realise a strong sexual experience. He couldn't resist. He composed with a frightening abandon. That is to say, the scene and the words simply tumbled on to the keyboard!

26.

August 19.
Simone,

Beware! Perhaps I have taken leave of my senses.

'Things were not good. I was in a foul frame of mind. More nonsense to contend with at work and therefore more energy wasted on the politics of life. Not even the glory of a post-work gym session had dampened my fury. All the gym had done was to prepare me more for the anticipated physical exertions that lay ahead. I drove off and found my way to the hotel. We had agreed to meet there. You had arrived. You were waiting in the lounge. We kissed but you were cold. I took your hand but you were cold. I smiled at you but you were cold. This was not good, I thought. This was my woman and she was treating me like a stranger. There were two ways to deal with this, I thought. This time I would take the less gentle one. We found our room. It was large. Two rooms in fact. We were left alone. Nothing was said. I checked the bedroom while you sat sullenly in front of the TV. This really was no use to me. My body was hard with anticipation. My mind was fired for love. But the route of conquest had now been settled upon and conquest I would achieve.

I needed to relax a little. I offered you a shower or at least least the request of your company. You declined. This was unusual. I asked what was wrong. Nothing! Fine, I thought. I shall carry on until I am fully satisfied. I showered with lingering pleasure, thinking about what I wanted to do. I am going to take you, my love, whether you like it or not, whether you enjoy it or not, whether you struggle or not, whether you condemn me or not, whether you cry out with pleasure or not.

My body glowed from the warmth of the shower. My face was smooth with the delicacy of my wet shave. My after-cream had sealed the smoothness. My towelling robe was damp yet warm. I wore nothing else. You noticed me and shivered slightly. "What's wrong, my love?" I asked again.

You said, "nothing," and just continued to stare at the TV. Something was wrong but you were clearly not going to share your thoughts with me. So I was going to have to ride the thoughts out of you. The bed was a large four-poster. Lots of room for moving and playing and if so inclined, tying and struggling. I stood in front of you and blocked the TV.

"Don't do that, John," you said. I turned it off.

"John!"

"Look at me!" I commanded.

You glanced up. I smiled a little but you responded with absolute non-interest – no engagement, nothing. I didn't understand but my last offer of reasonableness was over.

I took your hand to encourage you. You pulled away sharply. I took your wrist and held it firmly.

"You're hurting me!"

"I don't mean to hurt you. Just come with me!"

"No!" you said.

I took your other wrist and pulled you up to me, your face close to mine. Still no smile or response. I pulled you to the bedroom and looked at you again – no reaction. I threw you on to the bed. You tried to get up. I let you. I asked "why?" No answer. I tried to kiss you. You turned away. That was the final insult.

I threw you down and leapt on top. You started to struggle. I kissed you. You forgot yourself and started to respond. You realised and stopped, turning your head away. You began pushing me off. I took a silk cord from my pocket and lashed your wrist with it and, while you were struggling, tied it to the bedpost. You were becoming violent in reaction. I pinned you down and managed to tie your other wrist to the other bedpost. Your top half was now secure! Your legs were thrashing about. I kissed and licked your ears. The birth of sensuality appeared. The lure of your being partially tethered let me take your ankle and tie it firmly to the bottom post. The remaining leg tried vainly to work everything free. It was soon secured as well. I sat on my knees between your legs just resting a little and looking at you. Nothing had altered your apparent indolence. Why? I wondered but had given up asking. Your clothes were still on! I opened your blouse from the front and your bra from the front also. In this context, the almost lurid quality of your breasts was revealed. I savaged one with my mouth and tongue. I bit the nipple. You started to moan. I took the other and did the same. You responded some more, then called out, "You bastard!"

I stopped in my tracks. "What?" I said.

"You heard me!" And from that moment I heard nothing but the animal signals from within me needing to conquer and satisfy my need and desire for you. My avarice took hold.

I came off the bed and let my bathrobe go. I revealed my full erection to you. You looked fearfully. I moved up to your head and kissed it. The hair was delicate. I messed it up. I moved to your mouth and opened it with my fingers. I thrust my tongue in and found yours. You responded slightly. I was becoming fearsome in my energy and passion. I wanted my woman and I wanted her hard. I lunged to you and thrust my head in between your legs, my ass now staring you in the face, just out of your reach! I sucked and pushed. I could taste your sumptuous secretions starting. You wanted to be untied. You pulled at your arms but nothing gave way. I grabbed a pillow and thrust it under your ass. It elevated you and allowed for more oral penetration. I thrust my tongue in and out like a machine – very fast and with much liquid lubrication. You started to cum. I kept going. You moaned some more. I moved out, turned round and pushed two fingers into you. I started finger-fucking you. The speed was like that of me masturbating hard. You were being taken to a different level of orgasm.

"Untie me, John!" Then, "Ah, that is so beautiful," you cried. I stopped and took my cock, slapped it against your upper thigh, then positioned it, checked your moistness and plunged myself deep into you. I held that initial thrill for both of us, then started pumping. I wanted to satisfy you (and thereby, overcome your sullenness). I also wanted to eradicate yet more work frustrations. But most important of all, I just wanted to take my woman. I gripped your tied arms for extra leverage.

I thrust myself with gritted teeth and power. You writhed and called out. Fear and your next coming were entwined. We both fucked each other – you a little, me a lot. We started to cum in a crescendo of expletives. I lay there a moment, staying inside you, letting the final surges devour the inside of you. I gathered myself.

You spoke to me softly. I kissed you and moved to your arms. I untied you. You expected the wrists to be released. I quickly tied your wrists again, turned you round and strapped you to the crossbar at the bottom of the bed. I re-tied your legs, this time to the bottom of the two legs, your legs wide apart. You had no lateral movement. I came round and inspected your suspended frame, your beautiful back glistening with the light moisture of perspiration. I knelt down and started licking your ass – one cheek, then the other. I took your cheeks and pulled them apart to reveal the healthy pink glow of your asshole. I licked and sensed your spasm of shock and anticipation – rimming. I pushed hard with my tongue; you moaned and writhed a little. I sat down and turned around, staring at your pussy. You could fuck my face if you wanted. I licked your pussy, opening its lips to reveal the pink and moist beauty of it all. You were aroused again. I moved round and pushed a finger into you. I pulled out, positioned and pushed two fingers in. You were very wet again and your surly disposition had disappeared.

"Oh, John! John? Untie me, please untie me?"

I sat up on the end of the bed, my head at breast level, my mouth able to nibble on your erect nipples. I bit. You screamed with pleasure.

"In God's name, please untie me, John." I wanted to relent but found myself just savouring that moment of total domination. I moved my hands up the inside of your arms. You thought release was imminent. I tickled, then licked, your armpits and upper arms. I was erect again. My legs rested against your inner thighs. My manhood was exposed with its pink head, vibrating with desire. I shifted slightly and pulled you towards me. My manhood was getting close to your navel. I got you into place. I could resist no longer. I untied your legs. You brought them up and wrapped them around my waist. I untied your arms; they fell on to my shoulders. You held me around my neck. You pulled my rampant cock into yourself. We were now entwined. No. We were galvanised, completely locked in each other's passion.

We sat in a beautiful embrace. No movement – just the stillness of involuntary surges. We kissed gently and deeply. Our tongues danced together. I whispered in your ear.

"I love you so much. Never leave me! Please never leave me!"

You pulled your head back and looked deep into my eyes. You then kissed one, then the other. "I will never leave you, my beautiful man. I am yours forever." I shuddered with the depth and power of such simple words. I moved to your ear again and whispered softly.

213

"I'm sorry if I was too harsh with you! I needed you! I was hungry for you. Your denial threw me into a frenzy! You see, you have full control over me! My heart is totally yours!"

"Shush my love! Only you can take me like this!" As we spoke, we could feel just the slightest movements sending shivers of ecstasy through our one united body. You started to ride me; I started to respond. Your hands moved behind as you propped yourself up on the end of the bed. I took your breasts, squeezed and kissed them. I played with your nipples. I needed to hold you again. I lunged forward and took you in my embrace. You wrapped your arms around me once more. We could feel the cum arriving. It was slow and wonderful.

"Oh my god!" I shouted. "Oh my god! I love you so much. I love you so, so much! I am yours. I want to be yours for all time."

You held me close as we both started to spasm and spill our pleasure into each other. You screamed.

"Oh my love my precious love. Never leave me!" and as our surges abated our words of love and passion mingled into a generality of sustained joy and pleasure. We were jointly assuaged.

As we finished, I asked "what was wrong earlier?".

"Nothing my angel" you said. "I just wanted to see how badly you wanted me and how hard you would fight to take me! You are mine John! You are mine!"

As you whispered these words, you kissed me softly and we stayed entwined and penetrated.'

John,
You and only you can take me this way. I love you!

This was an interesting response for two reasons. First, it was brief, so brief that it carried no real meaning. Brevity was to be applauded but this was, in essence, nothing. Secondly though was the tell-tale phrase for a man who was basically insecure in all emotional matters. 'You and only you can take me this way.' The implication, of course, was that others could take her in other ways and maybe did. This train of thought was, yet again, infantile. Was she, in fact, a prolific lover. Anders had been around. She had alluded to other possibilities but again, what on earth was he getting into a flummoxed frame of mind for? This was neither bemusement or bafflement. He was perplexed and for all rational beings reading this he had absolutely no right to be so!

27.

August 26.

Sweet John,

I miss you! I think of you enjoying your vacation and running around with your kids and my heart warms with thoughts of you being content and happy under the sun on a lovely beach. I am so happy that you are in my life now; I have time to reflect on your pure existence into mine. What a wonderful and beautiful being you are, John. You are so adorable and so lovable and so special to me. My days are running very, very fast! Today I went for a haircut. My hairdresser is an Arab – originally from Jordan. He is such a sweet man. He told me much about his family concerns, about losing his wife to another man and having to care for his two-year-old girl. I felt so very sorry for him as he is usually a happy, cheerful man.

We celebrated my birthday yesterday and it was very nice! We all had a great time and my husband was very nice and sweet to me. It is great for us to remain friends and to care for each other still. Under the veil of so many disputes we still care for each other.

Time is running, John. It is running really fast. I will write more but for now... I miss you so terribly.

Simone.

August 27.

Dearest John,

I attempted reading your early e-mails to me and I just filled up with so much sadness. John, I need you. I log in my mailbox and it is empty of your sweet, warm, loving words.

What a horrible thing I have done! I know what I have done, John, I destroyed my family's life. I messed up my family and tore it apart. I am so numb with so much pain. I cannot, I really cannot live this death any more. I am so confused. I see time pass by and I cannot stop it. I feel so helpless. How will I sustain myself after Zak is gone? How will I walk through the house and not hear his voice; not see his twinkling eyes, his wicked laugh after mischief. I am so, so helpless. I cannot sleep any more. I just cannot sleep and all night I wake up and wait for the morning to come. I feel I have split personalities – the tormented soul inside, the strong manager during the day. I worry if I let my weakness seep through the crack of this iron mask of false cheerfulness I would drown in my sorrow. Come soon, John. I feel that I am losing my strength without your warm words.

Simone.

August 28.

Darling,

I miss you so much! There is something about you that is so nourishing and so vibrant to my whole being. Your words are so soothing. I re-read some of your e-mails again and I feel better – much better. Usually the morning is better than the night. At night I weaken a bit and fall prey to my dark thoughts as I struggle to sleep. I am fine this morning.

You must be having a great time with your family. How wonderful it is to be at a beach and enjoy the beauty of the sun and sand. I miss you so, so terribly. Do you think of me! Do you tell yourself 'My god, what is this connection all about! I do not understand it?' Do you look at your wife and children and get filled with happiness even though deep inside you wonder about what the future will bring them? Do not worry, my love. Only happiness and safety is coming your way. You shall rise again and you shall be happy.

Simone.

August 29.

My sweet John,

It is five in the morning. I woke up at three and just cannot go back to sleep. For the past few nights I tossed and turned and again tossed and turned. I miss you a lot. I just cannot believe the vacuum you have left behind. I read your e-mails and miss you even more.

Simone.

August 29.

My sweet darling angel,

Do you think of me. Are you happy? Darling, I do miss you so badly. I miss your warm loving presence in my life. I miss your caring all-consuming words. I miss your protection and advice. Darling, I want to feel your love gently caressing me. Where are you now?

Simone.

August 31.

Simone,

So many yearning messages, you beautiful woman!

Family holidays are interesting things. For northern Europeans with young children, it usually means two weeks in some sun-soaked place with lots of sea and swimming pools – things we can't take for granted in our own climate. My body is now brown from head to toe – except for that tell-tale band around my middle. It just highlights the tan and how quickly it will fade, but it's still fun to acquire and fun while it lasts. The children are all happier having had some heat and been in the open air for the two weeks. The real point about the holiday is simply for the five of us to be in the same place at the same time for the whole period. We ate, slept and played together almost the entire time. Graham found a friend and tended to veer off on his own at times. We had some tension – his will against that of the family and he's only ten! Moira continues to develop – now six. Andrew operates in his own disjointed world. He's four. If only… but nothing is perfect in this world except for the lucky few. Heather and I even had a little time for each other and at some points could have found ourselves making love if only for the tiredness of each day's exertions and the impracticality of the sleeping arrangements; I slept with Andrew in a separate room so that the other three could have uninterrupted sleep. In the end therefore, nothing was consummated. I suppose if I had really wanted it, it would have happened.

You see, my hope is that through our relationship, I might release some of my blockages domestically (some might say depression but I've never asked an expert). All I know is that I came to a point of desperate need. You heard the call and since then the embers of various things have been inflamed in different ways. So for this fleeting moment of seriousness, let me repeat – I really am touched and grateful that you have stuck with me!

You are tired and I must deliver you from such things. The pending emotional trauma is compounded. Please refrain from making those awful decisions that might be regretted. Make work decisions based on the enhancement of the firm, adding value and so on. Never be perceived as a negative force at work! Do not succumb to other temptations either. Be straight and true to yourself.

John.

August 31.

Dearest angel John,

It is so good to have you back! My goodness, it was so hard and I was so astounded at how precious and important your presence has become in my life. I relish in your thrill and excitement as I was of seeing you back online.

Your consummation of me gives me a warm blanket of cherished security and pleasure. You do not know how important you are to me. Your words and thoughts and everything about you is nourishing and stabilising to my spirit. You lift me up so easily and give me so much to look for. You excite me and thrill me and make laugh and happy. For that I am so grateful.

I do not know what exactly is happening between you and Heather. You mentioned that you rarely make love. I am amazed that with you having such passion and emotion and so much energy and yet you still do not share that with her.

What is this depression, my love? Do not listen to this! You are going through a phase in your life and surely you do have much to worry about and that is depressing. My love, do you feel that Heather is expecting more of you and you are helpless to deliver it? Do you talk about these things with her? Hang in there, John, and be patient with yourself and with her. You also have a house full of kids so intimacy usually suffers much disruption. It would be so beautiful if you and her could take time and make love gently and very romantically.

You must reach out to her and give her the happiness that she deserves. I am so sure that she is a beautiful woman inside and out. So much of the love that you give to me, you should also share it with her. She is much younger than you are so she needs more attention.

I wish so much to see you all happy and content and I pray for you to find peace and happiness.

At some point when I was thinking of you and Heather, I felt that it would be so beautiful if you were to make love to her. Just to think of such a thing makes me cherish you even more. Thinking of you giving her happiness and wrapping her with your affection is so precious. You are so wonderful, John! I do miss you so much.

As for why my marriage has come to this point? I do not really know if I can point to one reason. It is more of a state or process that evolves and over time where some precious things die. I am sad about the destruction of my family but happy about the end of my marriage. There are two levels, you know, in the death of a marriage. The adult relationship and the family unity are two different things. Our family relationship with the kids is wonderful. My husband is a wonderful, caring and loving father in every way and I am very loving of the children too. We have very happy moments as a family and the kids are happy and have fun as we play with them. When we resort to the adult relationship though, it is different.

I do not blame him. I think it is a mutual thing that led us to this point. It all started five years ago. The worst of it happened three years ago. We separated for four months and were on the path of divorce. We both felt terrible and, for Zak's sake, decided to give ourselves a chance. I met a gentleman at work and had an affair three years ago. That, I think, broke his heart. The affair did not even last three weeks. He found out and was very mad. He did some stupid things. We patched things up and moved on with our life, again for the family and to give ourselves a chance.

I am so happy that I found the strength to seek separation all the way through. It is a very hard decision because of the close family bonds. He is so attached to Zak, as I am, and to Sarah, as I am also. As for me and him? We care much about each other but we do not care enough. What do I want? Simply at this point, I do not know, but I do want to be loved and that I do not have in my marriage. Some people think it is naive to destroy a family for something so idealised. My coupled friends tell me that there is no such thing after marriage! There is no more idealized love. I am not sure. I have to stop now... the kids are up. I will catch up with you later, my love.

Simone.

September 4.

Simone,

Today was the return to a domestic reality. English children go back to school next week. We spent this morning with Graham, Moira and even Andrew, buying school clothes and shoes. The kids demanded food at noon so we stuffed hamburgers into them! They loved it! The afternoon saw Graham off with his friends. The rest of us went to a local country park. There is a small farm there too; animals that can be looked at and sometimes petted by innocent children. The weather was (and remains) lovely.

I spent much of the holiday thinking about the long-term future. I dread economic incapacity – even worse, poverty. I dread the idea of being old in a cold, damp climate like Britain. I cannot see myself moving into my declining years in such a place. I looked at the old Spanish people while we were on holiday. They won't have to fight to stay warm in winter, like I see many of our old people doing, wrapped in heavy coats, shuffling along. Heaven knows how the Russians have managed all these centuries. I thought about you and your climate and your location, looking at some of the pretty young Simones dancing about in the sunlight. I just wondered. But these are fantasies like our other more intimate ones to which we must return later!

John.

28.

September 7.

John,

I have scatterbrain fatigue syndrome. I call it SBF – really. I just cannot pull myself to write, think, do, sleep, eat, smile, and work. I simply want to float over the coming few days with the least amount of energy. I tried and tried to write you yesterday but I had no energy. I am sorry John.

Simone.

September 7.

My angel,

I felt negative waves coming from you, in terms of your struggle to cope with the pending awfulness of things. My darling, do not dissipate your energy on me when having to fight to maintain a sense of equilibrium for what is to come. Just hold on and, remember, no dark thoughts, please! Maybe we can talk on Thursday. Even if you are listless, maybe talking will help to unscramble some of this mess. But please, please, please, just keep going, my angel. I am with you on this!

John.

September 8.

Simone,

Forgive the following. I had another one of those so-psychic dreams (what are you doing to me?). Not two men this time – just one, the obvious one. What I still don't understand is that you are getting divorced. You are not in love with your husband any more. And yet (by your own telephone admission) you succumb, and it appears often to his physical needs and yours, presumably. A while ago you suggested that if you didn't care about it (if there was no emotion) then it's all right; yes? I think that's how it went. You fear temptation to satisfy your natural libido for the sake of the physical pleasure. You are therefore extremely conscious of that aspect of yourself. For that, you earn much credit as a person. Could it be though, could it just possibly be, that you are fighting signs of nymphomania? Just a thought; really, just a thought...

John.

September 8.

John,

Do not rush to conclusions. It is silly to throw away everything we built over a very outrageous comment of yours. I have to let it out of my system and understand your thinking behind the question. No, I am not a nymphomaniac! I am mad with you!

Simone.

John had committed the cardinal sin. Jealousy had entered his psyche and, with it, irrational thought. Two women (who

*cares); two men (still tormenting); but fucking her 'soon-to-be'
ex-husband and with pleasure. it seems, was too much for his
mind. What monumental foolishness on his side! He simply could
not understand his own reasoning. Maybe that was the point.
There was no reason. There was simple raw and, it seems, childish
emotion erupting. Was it that his maternal and sensual mother
figure was turning away from him, in his role as a child in need
of constant reassurance. If so, he had tapped into a feature of his own
psychological make-up that was deeply upsetting and potentially
devastating to a (very remotely possible) serious relationship in the
future. That was not his intention but it was a dimension to
himself that this relationship was now uncovering – and now he
had to face the consequences.*

September 9.

Simone,

I'm so sorry! I am quaking, not at my own stupidity (which
is bad enough) but at the thought that I am going to lose you.
I fear the worse already and am trying to brace myself for it.
Why, oh why, has this happened? I mean not in terms of your
reaction but what cosmic force compelled me into that line of
reasoning. It's as if a negative source has taken us over and we
are not able to influence it.

I shall stay silent after this unless or until you contact me
again, but I do fear the worst. It is ironic that I may have to 'close
down' my systems again until I recover from the loss. As you
know, emotionally, my only method of survival is to run away.
I am so sorry, Simone. So very sorry!

If you will accept just one piece of advice, it is that I think your decision to leave your marriage is correct but that the price is going to be heavy indeed. Ultimately though, your strength will prevail. You are just that type of person to survive. I envy that quality and ability in you! Please take care of yourself but contact me if you want to.

John.

September 13.

John,

The only difference is time; before and after. What I ended up with after you asked me that awful question is a total shutdown in my openness to you physically. I simply could not read that piece (again) for a whole day. I did not even touch it.

I think that will be my reaction to any sort of this type of writing for a while! I am sorry but I cannot help it. Am I strong? I am not so sure about that. I carry very deep scars from my marriage. My only crime was that I was successful in my career. My crime was that I sought success and worked very, very hard to be where I am. Yes, I will be strong. Please be strong too.

Simone.

September 14.

John,

Do not worry about us. I still do cherish you despite what you have done. I know it does not make any sense that I am still intimate with my (soon to be) ex-husband. I do not understand it either but if anything, yes, we do have a very strong bond despite all the hurt and all the pain.

Simone.

September 16.

Simone!

Thanks for not throwing me out (yet?). You are now part of my life and I would have serious problems (internally), if I actually lost you. And again, I do not think you are (that word). You are passionate but that is a different thing! The problem is to reconcile the divorce with the continued love-making. When I went through a similar process (splitting up after four years), sex with that person was the last thing on my mind. Again, I am very sorry indeed! I suppose I am descending to the conventional. I am actually becoming jealous. What stupidity; what infantile nonsense. What right have I to feel such a thing? None! So again, please forgive my momentary lapse.

John.

September 17.

Dear Simone,

I re-read your last message, word-for-word and everything there was to possibly encounter between the lines. I panicked. Your message sounds like a very gentle signing off. If so, I do not blame you. You are divorcing your husband and you make love to him. I am staying with my wife and I rarely make love to her. This is surely the ultimate contradiction! It is not you that is bad (when you talk of being accused of breaking up your family). It is me who is bad for failing to provide (unable to provide) that basic fulfilment for someone I love. So, I feel myself sinking right back to where I started on 21 May – just needing a friend, someone who might help me understand things more clearly.

Heavens! When I started, the most sensual thought I had (in terms of talking to a stranger) was being bathed! Look at how far and how deeply the exploration has taken us. It has certainly been a liberation for me and, for that, you have my gratitude eternally.

I am so, so sorry to have lost you. You remain deep down inside me. It is me that is bad, my angel. We need to turn the clock back a little!

John.

September 21.

John,

One can never go back to where one was. That is impossible. You told me once that a person can very much still love more than one person. If that is true, my only explanation for my dysfunctional marriage is that both my husband and I are not facing reality, but in time we will. One of us has to cut the cord and let go. Making love is a desperate attempt to avoid the inevitable fact (we are no longer together). Denial is such a powerful thing and love is such a strange animal.

Yes, I let myself float so freely with you and shut down all reason and all sense and opened windows of my soul to experiences I would never ever contemplate in real life. Our exchange caused you to think of me in terms that I opened myself to fit that description. I have gone from mad to disappointed, to hurt, to very sad and I stand today feeling very empty.

Maybe our last conversation is a good jolt of reality that we both needed. I deeply and truly love you still for everything that you are. I know that we can no longer continue this fantasy, this exploration. You know that too.

I sign off with a gentle kiss and a hug to you, my child, my lover, my angel. As I let you go, I kiss you again very gently and wish you love and happiness.

Farewell, my sweet darling angel. Remember me kindly and please kiss your little children for me, especially troubled Andrew.

Simone.

September 22.

Simone!

Oh no! That is not what I expected. It's such a devastating blow. All because of one foul and misplaced word. I really am so sorry, so very sorry. I think also my escape into this cyber-world adventure shall draw gracefully to a close. Without you, what's the point? I weep a little now.

John.

29.

For the next two weeks, John stared at the screen, devoid of all contact with Simone. He was having a hard time because of the loss of that external life that gave him momentum and spirit to deal with his own travails at home. Then suddenly...

October 6.
John.
Write me a romantic tale!
Simone

October 7.
Simone,
My god! I thought I had lost you. I understand a little more now, I think, and will try writing an emotional piece. I have a possible scenario in mind. I would never knowingly do anything to hurt you or to jeopardise us! Your understanding and your love is too, too precious to me. All my love (and I will leave you in peace at least until next Wednesday),
John.
P.S. I know the time is coming. Be brave, Simone,

and be strong for you are certainly strong.

P.P.S. A romantic tale? Nothing physical? Never tried! But I will for you! Help me if I falter. I thought our last conversation was evidence of an underlying bond. Crazy to say but no one knows me like you do. I have never shared such thoughts before. Take care of yourself for now. I'll be in touch, say, on Wednesday, to give you space (and me time to write). Finally, late October now remains a real possibility. Do you really think you will cope with an emotional me at that time? In other words, do I seriously start planning for that possible trip or not?

John.

October 9.

John,

Why do you ask me if you should plan a trip or not? Are you not sure of your desire to come? Part of me says yes I sure do want you to visit. The other part is confused. I think now that you do not know me. I sure do know you and understand you but I am not sure if you do see me and do know me. Life and our exploration are complex!

Simone.

October 10.

My love!

You are wise, even in your desperation. You are in pain, of two kinds – the rotten time of month and the pain of almost perpetual tears. You know I have been with you through all of this but have chosen not to raise the subject and therefore not to dwell on it. I decided that I would simply be here for you, to respond with love and support when you needed it and, therefore, when you called for it. This is also the subject that helped us develop – first our relationship and then our love. I am with you, dearest Simone. Just remain within yourself (no easy matter) but retain that inner strength and take comfort in the courage of your father – who helped break the mould for you (letting you marry an outsider).

Though it has ended in failure, you have emerged with freedom, intellect and a stunning career to come (as well as a stunning appearance now!). So, try and rest as best you can and just drop me little notes or snippets to let me know how you are, no matter how bad. Meanwhile, we *shall* plan for a visit on or around October 25th (Wednesday), with you off on Thursday and Friday and me with you till early the following week.

John.

October 11.

John,

If anyone needs to be asked how they manage, it is you. How do you manage to write so beautifully and so tenderly? Your words are pure magic. You make me smile through my darkest hours. I love your children, your wife, you and everything about your world.

Simone.

October 12.

My angel,

Last night I kissed my children good night and at one point consciously kissed each of them from you; it sent electricity through me each time. You send electricity through me! How do you manage that as I reel in the realisation that you are deep, deep inside me, and I want you to stay there?

Yes, NOW, you feel terrible but the decision was the correct one and once that pain subsides (and it will), you will find yourself soaring professionally, personally and emotionally. Just keep going, my beautiful Simone. Know that I am going to see you through this, then I am going to see you, then I am going to hold you, then I am going to comfort you, then I am going to love you, then I am going to make love to you and if we are lucky, I will drive you to distraction with the pleasure of it all!

John.

October 14.

My dear Simone,

I don't know what your state of mind is but I can imagine. I don't know how your heart is feeling but I can guess. I don't know how your tears feel but I can wonder! In all these things, I have nothing but care in my heart for you. I am with you. I thought of you last night as I fell asleep, wondering how you were going to manage today. You *will* manage. You *must* manage for, if no one else, yourself and your survival. Be strong, my angel, and fight your way through this next day or two. We have written of this on a few occasions. Each time I tried to build up your inner strength for the actual event. No, my love, just be strong… and contact me when you need to. I don't know about 'chatting' this evening. Domestic realities encroach, sometimes too much for my own liking. If I can, you know I will. Most importantly, you know I want to so, so much!

John.

October 15.

John,

I am slowly recovering… I talked to Zak yesterday and my child is such a wonderful spirit! He is so pure and so brave. He is happy and well-adjusted and loves his school and new teachers. He asked me to come and visit his new house. He now says "mommy's house" and "daddy's house" to differentiate between the two. Overall, he is doing really well. I miss him like crazy... each time I see a four-year-old child I almost burst into tears. I am in a very bad emotional state. I brace myself to see the good things in this, rather than the bad, but I cannot help feel frighteningly sad to the point of sickness in my stomach.

Simone.

October 15.

Simone,

Apart from my wife, you are the bravest woman I know. Time is the great healer! Your message and our brief chat, signals to me that you need time to heal yourself internally. I am therefore going to leave you in peace until you are ready to resume our friendship. My channels of communication will remain open...

John.

October 15.

John,

Can you access your mail? I am going through the worst time in my life ever. I have not thought the pain will be this much nor the heartache. It is like constant fire burning inside of me and I miss Zak to the point of destruction. I am so, so miserable.

Simone.

October 16.

John,

Where are you? I have not heard from you for a long time now. I have been struggling really hard and I am still trying to cope with my new life. I am very depressed. Let me know how you are doing if you have a minute to spare.

Simone.

30.

October 20.

Simone,

'The room was comfortable, just like in a decent hotel. The one secret was the contents of the drawers and what lay behind the cupboard doors. The agreement was that you were to "do with me what your erotic and fetish-strewn heart desired." The three conditions were no other men involved, no gagging (I simply want to use words, even harsh words) and, when I indicated 'enough', that really meant 'enough!'

You sat in the soft chair, already naked, playing superficially with your pussy. You ordered me to stand in front of you.

"Take your clothes off, slave!"

I did, one by one, until I was naked. My erection was already sound.

"Move closer to me!"

I did. You took my cock in your hand and inspected it. You lingered as you formed your right hand into a tube that gripped the top half of my manhood. You pulled the foreskin back a little, then forward, then back, then forward and back, back and back again until there was nowhere else for it to go. The pink-purple head was glistening already with pre-cum. You moved to the front of your seat and took my cock into your mouth. You fucked me with your mouth, moving your other hand to my balls. You caressed and gently massaged them. I began to feel the start of explosion. You withdrew.

"Masturbate, you bastard! Spurt it on to my face, you fucking animal!"

I started to capture the initial excitement of your sucking. My arm began to tighten with effort. My body became taut. You touched my stomach and felt it to be hard. You sat back and motioned for me to ejaculate on to your face. I kept the friction going with speed, moved closer, began to feel the eruption and took aim. "Cum on to me! Pour it on to me!" With that I shot my first burst, splatting on to your face, around your nose and upper lip. The next spurt shot into your open mouth. The pouring became lazier and dripped on to your breasts and front generally.

"Lick it off, slave! Now!"

As you tasted a little around your mouth, I started to lick and consume my own sperm from every portion of your body it had covered. Your nose was licked clean. I pushed my tongue into each nostril as well for good and delicious measure. Your mouth was consumed. I moved to your upper chest and tasted some more. I left your breasts till last – then, as I licked, I took hold of each nipple between my teeth. I bit to the point that you felt it.

You took me by the hair and pulled me away. I was still on

my knees.

"Move to the end of the bed on your knees and put arms forward."

I did. You took each wrist and bound them, then pulled one to the right, the other to the left. You moved to the end with bars and tied my wrists firmly so that they were attached; my arms pulled in front of me like a 'Y'. My torso lay on the bed, my head turned to one side for comfort. My ass pointed out from the end of the bed; I was still kneeling. You left for a moment. You came back with a black leather swimsuit garment on. It stopped at your pubic hairline. Your pussy and asshole remained exposed. You wore an eye mask. You carried a whip. You showed yourself to me, then climbed on to the bed. You stood astride my back, facing towards my ass, then sat. I could feel the gentle moistness from you on my back. You took the whip and tickled my ass. You removed it. I heard the air cracking with your next motion. I tensed myself.

"Keep still, you male whore!" Your next motion saw the whip tails strike my ass with a force that made me just conscious of what real fear might be like. You did it again and again, each time my body tensing as if the worst would happen and I would cry out with pain. There was no pain, just awareness. You bent down and bit my right ass cheek, then the left. That was more painful. You moved off me and off the bed, round to my back. You started to use the whip again, this time on my back. I did not like it. You could sense it and you stopped. It wasn't sore the way you had done it, but the fear was palpable. You fell to your knees. I waited a second, then felt lubrication being administered around my asshole. You pushed a finger in and out; you pushed pushed two in. I reacted slightly. You felt the tightness.

"Relax, slave, because you are going to be fucked!" The whip handle had its slight bulge at its end. You dipped it into the lubrication, then, without warning, pushed it into me so that the bulge was lodged inside.

"Bastard!" I called out.

"How dare you speak like that." You motioned the handle in and out of me a few times. You tested the possibility of speed. It worked and was, in fact, easier for me. You left it there and disappeared. You came back. You pulled the handle out and, before I knew it, you were pushing a rubber cock into me, strapped to you. You lay on your front, on top of my back. You were thrusting with your stomach muscles, pumping into me as if you were a man. "How do you like it, whore? How do you like being fucked like a woman is fucked?" As you asked, you stretched forward with your arms and gripped me as close to my wrists as you could reach. As you gripped, you fucked me until you were exhausted.

You then lay on me with the penetration still real. You recovered and pulled yourself away. You stood and moved to the bed end and untied my wrists. "Get on to the bed and turn on your back!" No sooner had I done so than you tied me up again, by the wrists, and, this time, by the ankles to the bottom end. The famous figure 'X' was now in place. You were still in your black leather outfit and eye mask. You took my cock in your hand and worked it to the point that it was ready to fuck anything that moved. It stood hard and erect.

You moved astride me and lowered yourself full-square on to my welcoming manhood. You let that first penetration surge through you. You then moved into your own thrusting action.

"Tell me I'm beautiful! Tell me I am the most beautiful ride you have experienced! Tell me!" you pleaded.

"Every time we fuck, it is the fuck of a lifetime. You are the best whore in this world. You are delicious!"

As I spoke, you fucked yourself into a frenzy, until you collapsed on me in a heap, crying with the surges inside you. It was enough.

You recovered and untied me – arms and legs. The game wasn't over as you had thought though. I was tired of being the subordinate creature. I waited till I sensed that you were whole again. I stroked your hair and head as if gentleness was about to ensue. Then you gasped as my grip on your hair tightened.

"Get off the bed and move your ass!" I pulled you to the bathroom and stood you against the wall of the shower. I let my grip go, took your arm and turned you round. I pressed you against the wall and inspected the garment you wore. The zip was at your back. I unclasped the top, then pulled the zip down unceremoniously. The leather fell to the front. I took off the eye mask. I kicked both things away and spun you around. I took hold of your hair again and pushed you to your knees. I positioned your face to be close, to feel the oncoming jet. I warned you, then started to piss in your face. You tried to move away.

"Stay still, you fucking whore!" I held you and let the

piss spray onto your hair, then over your face again, before giving your breasts a covering. I emptied myself upon you. I finished.

I pulled you up and sat down, where the piss was slowly ebbing away.

"Your turn, whore, and do it well!"

You stood up and moved astride. I kept a grip of your outer thighs and cheeks, making sure that you realised that I was still in control. You strained a little, then started. As you did, I pushed my middle finger into you and let the piss flow along my arm and on to my shoulder. I withdrew and let you empty yourself upon me. As you dripped your last droplets, I stroked you with gentleness. We were now both thoroughly covered in this golden wonder. I stood and turned on the lovely jets from the shower. We became clean again and as we did, we washed each other with great care – front and back, up and down, in and out. We were delightfully and completely finished. We moved back to the bed, our bodies dried and delicately powdered. We climbed into bed and held each other closely. You snuggled your face into the nape of my neck. Before I knew it, you were sleeping like a baby. I held you and wondered why I was so lucky to share such things with you with total trust and complete (well, almost complete) abandon. As I lingered on such thoughts and my love for you, built from erotic pleasures and total trust, I drifted into a rapturous slumber, letting one hand linger around your beautifully delicious pussy.'

John.

31.

He re-read his latest creation the following morning and realised that he must have taken leave of his senses. She asked for a tender and loving tale. He sent her this! Was he sick or was he just trapped in the mind-set of a child, wanting to play again and again with his favourite new toy and to seek reassurance? He soon found the answer.

October 27.

My sweet John,

I just finished reading your e-mail. I gasped a few times at the shocking details. My darling angel, what a troubled mess you have brewing inside your soul! Why such torment? Why such extremes? I think you want to be totally consumed by a woman. You are so childish. Yet, there is a deep, bitter darkness lurking inside you and it is tormenting you. You have a deep, deep frustration with the fact that you were abandoned by your mother. It is so strange but I feel the child in you reaching out all through your scenarios and, with strong tantrums, demanding attention. At the end of each scenario you are aching to be loved and you abuse yourself because you think that you are not worthy of love... but, my darling, you are! You are beautiful with your darkness and with your innocence. innocence.

You are going too far, my dear John, not only with me but also with yourself. Such dangerous ground we are venturing in to. I recognise the sure possibility of becoming emotionally 'screwed up' just by reading your scenarios. I need to know why you punish yourself so much. When you indulge in the S & M imagination you are really punishing yourself. I am here, John, to hear your voice... talk to me... open your soul... open your heart... you are truly safe.

Simone.

October 27.
Simone,
Subject to confirmation of my travels elsewhere, I could use up some airmails, arriving JFK Tuesday, 31 Oct, departing Tuesday, 7 November.

John.

October 27.
John,
I need some downtime for myself. Many thoughts race through my head and the amount of stress and pressure is overwhelming me now. I need a lot of time to think introspectively: who I am; what I want and where my life is going. I cannot communicate with you for a while so I can focus on myself. I truly apologise, but I feel my energy is wasted and I am very, very tired most of the time.

Take care, John, and I do pray that your life will take a turn to the best and brighter side of life.

Simone.

October 28.

Simone,

Let me now save you the bother of rejecting me as well as my traveling offer. I have just heard that I will not be available as planned. The gods (and you) are now not with us. Never mind. Just build your strength for your exciting new future and take care of yourself! Contact me again when you are ready – a week; a month; a year...

John.

She never did and, in truth, he had exhausted himself as well. More fundamentally, though, as he reflected on the whole experience, he realised that he was still a child. He had been introduced to maternal care and, eventually, to a new 'toy'. Then he wanted constant reassurance and affirmation from her that whenever he played with it, with her, he was still loved and wanted. In his adult guise, he wanted to be desired and hungered for, in the face of his need to conquer – at her behest! His was a selfish approach to Simone at a time when she was going through her crescendo of pain to its climax – the loss of her son. In mitigation, he was trying to reflect and explain that pain through his own experience: the loss in reverse – John's loss of his mother when he was five, just one year older than Simone's loss of Zak.

Yet, he had uncovered something in her that she was relishing (the desire to be conquered), until the point where he went too far. Curiously, that point was not the conquest of her (though she started cautioning against it) but the accusation that, in essence, she she couldn't say 'no'. In truth, it was a terrible accusation but jealousy contorts the most rational mind. What possible right had he to be jealous? No. 'Right' was the wrong word. What possible 'reason' could he have for being jealous? On the face of it, it was absurd. Yet his emotional turmoil from his earliest childhood years was now being uncovered. Matters would have to be resolved if he was to become a complete and well-rounded emotional being. On the other hand, it was an enriching experience. It was an exhilarating journey – a real exploration of things he had never contemplated before. What concerned him most of all was the realisation that he had tapped into something. It was not sinister. It was certainly erotic – at times, even pornographic. The point though was that his appetite had been whetted. He wanted to dream some more. He had to. There was so much still to uncover. There was a latent potential within him. His heart began to race in anticipation. He re-opened Yahoo Personals, where this all began. He drafted another advertisement. It was, again, centred on his autobiographical writing. It was, of course, a subtle ruse. He just wanted to re-enter the world of electronic dreams. No! In fact, he wanted to get deeper into the whole process of erotic dreams and maternal reassurance.

The End.